PRIMAL 2055
ESCAPE

JACK SILKSTONE

PRIMAL
2055
ESCAPE

JACK
SILKSTONE

vinci
BOOKS

By Jack Silkstone

PRIMAL 2055

PRIMAL 2055 — Escape
PRIMAL 2055 — Quest

The Primal Series

PRIMAL Origin
PRIMAL Unleashed
PRIMAL Vengeance
PRIMAL Fury
PRIMAL Reckoning
PRIMAL Nemesis
PRIMAL Redemption
PRIMAL Renegade
PRIMAL Deception
PRIMAL Exodus

SEAL

SEAL of Approval
SEAL the Deal
Signed SEAL'd and Delivered

Standalone

The Operative

Vinci Books

vinci-books.com

Published by Vinci Books Ltd in 2026

1

Copyright © Jack Silkstone 2017

The author has asserted their moral right to be identified as the author of this work in accordance with the Copyright, Designs and Patents Act 1988. This work is a work of fiction. Names, characters, places and incidents are the product of the author's imagination or are used fictitiously. Any resemblance to actual persons, living or dead, places and incidents is entirely coincidental.

All rights reserved. No part of this publication may be copied, reproduced, distributed, stored in any retrieval system, or transmitted in any form or by any means, including photocopying, recording, or other electronic or mechanical methods, nor used as a source for any form of machine learning including AI datasets, without the prior written permission of the publisher.

The publisher and the author have made every effort to obtain permissions for any third party material used in this book and to comply with copyright law. Any queries in this respect should be brought to the attention of the publisher and any omissions will be corrected in future editions.

A CIP catalogue record for this book is available from the British Library.

Paperback ISBN: 9781036703844

The EU GPSR authorised representative is Logos Europe, 9 rue Nicolas Poussion, 17000 La Rochelle, France contact@logoseurope.eu

Chapter One

The Institute, Jordan

The noise that woke her sounded like a hundred demons howling as they swept over the ramshackle hut. An explosion shook the mud-brick walls and the ground trembled. "Mother, mother!" the girl screamed, clutching a threadbare blanket to her chest.

Dust and debris fell from the rusted tin roof as the door to her room burst open and a figure appeared. It was a woman, with brown hair, angular features and dark almond shaped eyes, her mother. Strong arms grabbed her from the bed and held her tight.

Another explosion rocked the hut. She buried her face in her mother's hair as the crackle of gunfire penetrated the thin walls. Voices filled the air, terrified screams and people calling for loved ones.

Her mother led her out into the dark streets. More of the demons screamed and she glanced skywards, catching a glimpse of a flaming streak across the stars. Smoke and dust burnt her throat as they fled along streets where, earlier that day, she had played.

Others ran with them. She recognized the faces: shop owners, friends and neighbors. They wore masks of terror as they fled. More flames, more noise, more screams, but she was safe with her mother.

They reached the outskirts of the village and made for the river. Over her shoulder she saw fire spreading through the huts like a hungry animal, consuming all it touched. Cries carried in the air as flames leaped skyward.

"We'll be safe in the hills," her mother said as they joined a group of people on the riverbank.

She glanced up at the star that hung over the mountains. Her mother called it the Guardian Star. It would lead them to safety.

A tearing noise ripped across the river and people screamed, pushing back against them. As they shoved, bullets cracked through the air, but her mother stayed strong. She led her away, up the bank.

People fell as more gunfire sounded. She could hear the projectiles snap overhead and thump into the ground around them.

As they climbed she felt her mother shudder and let out a cry. Her usually firm grip failed, letting her hand slip. More bullets hissed around them as sharp claps sounded from the darkness. Her mother dropped to her knees.

She scrambled to her mother's side and grasped her face. Her skin was pale in the moonlight, eyes wide and sad. Blood trickled from the corner of her mouth. "Run," she croaked. "Run."

Bodies barged past as villagers fled from the violence. She clutched her mother as her beautiful eyes closed.

"Momma, momma," she cried, but there was no response as her body slumped to the ground.

A hand grasped hers and she looked up to see a face she recognized, the boy from the next street, her friend.

"Run! We need to run," he yelled, standing protectively over her.

She watched in horror as bullets struck him. He slumped forward, eyes wide.

She screamed as he crumpled to the ground. Scrambling to her feet she ran as fast as her legs would carry her, back toward the burning village, back to her home. People fled past as they tried franticly to escape the death and destruction.

At the outskirts of the shantytown she spotted figures. Armed men, their faces wrapped in scarves, lurked among the buildings. She watched in horror as they dragged a woman, kicking and screaming, inside one of the shacks. As she rounded a corner, she nearly collided with a group of them. One of them lunged at her and she fell backward. He kicked her and she doubled over in pain. Cruel laughter sounded over the gunfire and explosions.

Curling into a ball, she moaned softly, "Momma, momma." Rough hands yanked her from the ground.

"Your momma's dead, bitch" growled a voice.

A cord looped around her neck. She grasped it with her hands as it tightened, cutting into her fingers. Collared like a dog she was dragged past burning shacks and sprawled corpses.

By the time they reached the center of the village she was fighting for breath. She tried to scream when, in the flickering light of the fires, she saw men dangling from the tree she sat under on market days. More of the masked gunmen watched and laughed as legs kicked like frogs in a pond, faces contorted and eyes bulging.

Her breath came in short, frantic pants as the man who leashed her pushed her toward a shack. A terrified scream echoed from within and she bolted. The cord jerked around her neck, yanking her off her feet and onto her back. Then as she lay in the dust, clawing at the rope, she heard a familiar sound.

Rounds snapped through the air. Her captor let out a grunt and fell in front of her, his face split like a ripe summer melon. Grey flesh and blood mingled with the earth.

Cries filled the air as more gunmen collapsed, but she didn't hear them as she gasped for breath.

As she fought to stay conscious, something cut the cord. Soft plastic touched her mouth and cool fresh air filled her lungs.

The man that knelt over her wore a helmet with a faceplate that was raised. She could see his eyes. Brown, they reflected the flames.

"Hostile targets destroyed," said a strange metallic voice.

She glanced out of the corner of her eye and spotted a black, vaguely human shape standing a few yards distant. Its arms and legs looked like tubes. Its head turned toward her. In place of eyes it had a cluster of lenses. It seemed to be studying her.

"Sweep the village and provide medical aid to anyone still alive," said the man, in a clipped voice.

There was a whirr as the humanoid machine disappeared into the darkness.

"You don't need to be afraid," he said, lifting her effortlessly from the ground. He made a mechanical noise, not unlike the robotic figure as he carried her across the market square.

She looked up from his arms as something roared above them. A dark shape blocked the stars as it flew overhead, twin blue flames trailing as it passed.

The man carried her past more of the black robotic figures and out into the desert where the aircraft had landed. The clean air she breathed from the facemask calmed her as she was carried under black wings, up a ramp and into the glowing inside. He laid her on a stretcher attached to the bulkhead.

A new face appeared, a woman with bright blue eyes.

"Momma?" she murmured behind the mask.

"You're safe now child. You're safe now."

She sat upright, tearing the mask from her face. "Where's my momma?"

"It's OK." The woman pushed her gently back against the bed.

Tears streamed from her eyes and panic assailed her. "No! Momma, I want momma."

She felt a sting on her arm then suddenly she was falling, sucked into a black void that engulfed her. "Momma, momma…"

She woke in a panic, fingers clutching at her face, searching for an oxygen mask that wasn't there. It took her a moment to realize where she was. Her breathing slowly returned to normal as she lay, staring at the dark ceiling. "Lights," she ordered.

The ceiling illuminated, filling the room with a soft glow.

She sat up, swung her legs off the bed and padded the few feet to a desk.

The tiny room had been her home for six months, the same period that she had been experiencing the re-occurring dream. Her childhood was something she could not remember. A Sakkin doctor had told her it was because of the trauma she had endured. Her underdeveloped emotions had chosen to forget what she could not process.

She pulled a plastic stool from under the desk then climbed onto the sleek white surface. Reaching to the ceiling she displaced one of the incandescent panels. She withdrew a small tattered notebook, replaced the panel, climbed down and sat at the desk. The book was technically her only possession. Everything else in the room, from the toiletries to the fitted black uniforms that hung in her cupboard, belonged to Sakkin Industries, the company whose operatives had rescued her from the men in her dreams.

She slid a pencil from the notebook's spiral binding and flicked through the worn pages. Inside were sketches from her dreams. Finding the next empty page she worked fast to capture the details before they faded from memory. It took a matter of moments to finish. Lowering the pencil, she examined what she had drawn.

From the paper gazed a beautiful woman with high cheekbones, almond eyes and flowing brown hair. It was a sketch of the lady from her dreams, her mother.

Lifting her head, she studied the face in the mirror attached to the wall. She had the same bone structure, but her eyes were more Asiatic. She was darker than her mother, her skin smooth and brown, free from the damage of the sun. She could not remember the last time she had walked outside, uncovered. The doctors said she was sixteen years old. All she could remember was the short time she had been at this training school, known as the *Institute*.

Closing her eyes she ran her fingers through her hair, desperately trying to recall the smell and feel of her mother. But, as always, the memory had faded leaving her with nothing other than the sketch. A tear ran down her cheek and she flicked back through the pages, searching for more memories.

The notebook was filled with sketches: a picture of the man who saved her, the boy who had been killed and even a map of her village. These images were the only link she had to her past. The only hope she had of ever finding her people and possibly, her father.

He had never appeared in any of her dreams. That meant there was a chance that he was still alive. Her gaze returned to the mirror and studied her reflection. Given her Eurasian features, it was likely that her father was of Asian descent. She had often wondered why he was not in the village that night. Had he left them, or had he passed away? They were questions that she asked on a daily basis.

A soft chiming sounded and the light panels increased in intensity.

"Good morning trainee Eight Two," a soft feminine voice filled the room. "Your first training session is in the unarmed combat facility at zero seven thirty."

Eight Two was her unique identifier. Every Sakkin trainee had one. She'd had a real name once, she was sure of that. Her mother had used it in a dream. However, on waking it had melted from her memory. No matter how hard she tried, she had never been able to recall it. So, for now, she remained Eight Two.

Touching the mirror she changed it to a digital display. "Show my timetable."

She glanced at the list of classes before climbing back onto the desk and returning her notebook to its hiding place. Then she showered in the tiny bathroom at the rear of the room and donned one of the sleek black uniforms that hung in her wardrobe. Slipping her feet into a pair of combat trainers, she pulled them tight and rose from the bed. She found her smart watch on the desk and slid it onto her wrist. A glance in the mirror confirmed her hair was in a regulation-sized bun. Then she slapped her palm against a biometric lock and the door snapped open.

Outside, the sterile white corridor rang with footsteps. Eight Two waited for a group of like-uniformed students to pass and then slipped in behind them.

It was a short walk to the dining facility. On the way, she passed a half-dozen more doors to rooms exactly like hers. One of them snapped open and a fellow trainee stepped into the corridor and nearly collided with her.

"Good morning," she said pleasantly.

The teenager stared at her but did not say a word. Turning he jogged after the group ahead, leaving Eight Two alone in the corridor. She sighed and followed them into the dining room.

Ten other corridors merged in the circular room that served as their dining hall. Each one had twelve rooms, giving the facility a maximum capacity of one hundred and twenty trainees. However, her class of forty was currently the only one. Most of those were already seated and eating at the tables that ran out from the central food distribution point. She walked to it, found a spare screen, selected her meal choices and waited. A split second later the replicator ejected a tray with a squirt of mushy gray nutrient paste and a juice box. Taking the tray she turned and searched for a seat.

This was the part she dreaded most, finding somewhere to sit where she could eat her breakfast in peace. In the last few months she'd come to realize that she was not like the others. For a start she was female, most of them were teenage boys, orphans from the Greater Middle Eastern Conflict. But there was something else, something far harder to define. It was as if her entire class of forty trainees was completely devoid of emotion. Each one was cold, ruthless and utterly unapproachable.

She spotted an empty table and made a beeline for it. Sitting she shoveled the soy based replifood into her mouth without making eye contact with any of the others.

"Mind if we join you?"

She recognized the voice as belonging to one of the four teenage boys who were part of her squad. Glancing up she locked eyes with Three Three, the self-appointed leader of squad *Gurion*. At six foot, he stood a full six inches taller than her and was at least thirty pounds heavier. The other members had taken to calling him Tree. His eyes were dark brown to the point of being black and he wore a permanent grimace on his chiseled features. The other members of the squad stood alongside him, four sixteen year olds that looked so similar they could have been brothers.

"I said, mind if we join you?" said Tree gruffly as he sat and shoved her tray out of the way.

The others followed suit crowding in around her.

Tree eyed her tray then reached across and grabbed her juice. "You know what they say. A team that eats together wins together."

"I've never heard that before," Eight Two said quietly.

He finished the juice and tossed it back on her plate. "Then you heard it here first."

"Seniors on deck," bellowed a voice.

Eight Two and her colleagues leaped to their feet, snapped their arms to their sides and stared directly ahead. From the corner of her eye she spotted two members of the senior class circling the room like sharks. The eighteen year old males were only months away from graduating from the *Institute*. They moved with a deadly grace, not unlike the tigers that Eight Two had seen during her global immersion classes.

One of them turned into their aisle shoving chairs aside as he made a beeline for them. He was a few inches shorter than Tree, but his chest, arms and shoulders were considerably more developed. His dark eyes were narrow giving the impression that he was always squinting.

Eight Two knew who he was. His designator started with the numerals Seven Nine Nine. Three numerals showed that he was in his final year of training and was to be treated with the necessary respect.

"Are you squad *Gurion*?" he asked in Arabic.

Tree nodded.

She felt the senior's eyes linger on her. "Is this girl one of yours?"

He nodded again.

Eight Two felt a flush of color in her cheeks as Seven Nine Nine examined her from head to toe. His lip curled into a scowl and he gestured to the team. "Don't you have somewhere to be?"

"YES, SIR!" yelled Eight Two and her teammates.

As they turned to leave, Seven Nine Nine grabbed Tree by the arm. "Not you."

Tree stood like a statue as his teammates and the other trainees made their way to the bank of elevators located on the curved dining room wall.

Seven Nine Nine watched the trainees enter the elevator

in an orderly fashion. "I've been allocated *Gurion* for the *Tsalmaveth*." He turned and locked eyes with Tree. "It's your job to make sure they are ready."

He swallowed. "Yes, sir."

"That girl is a weakness. Weakness must be removed before it cripples the team. Now, go."

Tree snapped into action and strode across to the elevators where the last of his class were filing inside. The doors closed with a quiet hiss. As the high-speed capsule rose, he smirked.

Chapter Two

The Institute, Jordan

Eight Two adjusted the side straps on her torso armor then twisted from side to side. Satisfied it didn't inhibit her movement she made to don the soft head armor that trainees wore during unarmed combat training.

"You won't be needing that," a gruff voice declared.

She turned to face the instructor who stood in the center of one of the *Institute's* unarmed combat labs. He was dressed in the jet-black fatigues worn by the facility's staff.

"The stakes have been raised," he said as he paced the rubber fighting mats. "From now on all of your unarmed combat will be performed without head gear. Fighting through the haze of concussion is something you will learn to endure. Now, fall in."

Eight Two dropped the headgear and stepped into line at the edge of the mat with the rest of squad *Gurion*.

"Today you will fight four two-minute rounds, full

contact until submission," announced the man. He took a flexipad from his pocket and studied the screen.

Eight Two felt a wave of apprehension sweep over her. By far she was the smallest in the team. Even the lightest of the four boys had at least twenty pounds and four inches of reach on her. Without the protection of headgear there was a real chance she could be injured, or worse.

The instructor eyeballed the team. "First fight, Three Three and Eight Two."

Her heart skipped a beat as Tree stepped forward. She followed his lead and tentatively moved onto the mat as the instructor stepped to one side.

"Standby," he ordered, fingers tapping on the flexipad.

Eight Two moved to the yellow square marked on the floor and turned to face her opponent. Tree grinned menacingly as he took up a fighting stance.

She exhaled and adopted a more relaxed posture. The white paneled walls of the combat lab began flashing. A number 5 appeared and a shrill beep sounded as the numbers counted down:

4.

3.

She exhaled slowing her heart rate as she stared directly at her opponent's throat.

2.

Tree's body tensed. She focused on remaining calm.

1.

He launched at her a split second before the call.

"FIGHT!"

As Tree lunged the white walls changed to combat video footage. Rock music and explosions blasted from hidden speakers. It was designed to add complexity and intensity to the situation, overwhelming the combatants' senses.

Eight Two ducked under Tree's right cross and dove to the opposite side. He moved with lightning speed, but she knew from previous sessions that she was faster. His power was the greatest threat. Without her head gear all it would take was one solid blow and she was finished. Spinning she faced her opponent as he launched another attack. Once again she ducked under his punch, but this time she counter punched, aiming for his armpit.

Both fighters wore reactive low profile armor over their combat uniforms. Soft and pliable it hardened to defeat blows from weapons and projectiles.

Eight Two struck like a cobra, knife-handing the tendons under his arm. He grunted and lashed out with a kick as she weaved past. The blow caught her armor, sending her flying into the mat.

Tree let out a roar and she rolled sideways to avoid his boot. Flipping cat-like onto her feet she followed up with a volley of kicks. The blows landed on his torso with seemingly little effect. She switched target to his face, with a lightning fast sidekick that snapped his head back.

Tree staggered and shook his head. Eight Two paused as she evaluated the effectiveness of the blow. She was breathing hard with sweat dripping from her brow. As she considered following up with another attack a buzzer sounded, indicating the end of the first round.

The two fighters moved back to their designated squares as the walls went blank and the rock music subsided. Eight Two closed her eyes and exhaled as a soft feminine voice counted down to the next round. When it reached five seconds, she wiped her brow and opened her eyes, staring calmly at her opponent.

"I'm going to crush you like a bug," he growled, his face running with sweat.

Eight Two smiled pleasantly as the countdown hit one and the voice announced, "FIGHT."

The rock music and videos returned as they approached the center of the mat. Tree moved more cautiously now. She knew she'd shaken him with that last kick. He wouldn't make any rushed mistakes. If she was going to win it needed to be a knock out blow and in the next two minutes.

She circled, searching for a gap in his defense.

Tree launched a powerful front kick followed by a left and right cross. She managed to side step, throwing her armored forearms up to block the punches. His assault drove her back toward the wall, until she finally broke sideways.

He turned and followed, sweat streaming from his face as he threw another barrage of punches. Eight Two ducked and weaved then struck out with a kick. It missed his groin, landing on his thigh. Tree staggered, then slipped on the sweat-slicked floor and fell, whipping his head against the rubber mat.

A savage kick to the face would have ended the fight, but Eight Two waited for him to rise. Dazed he made it to his knees, struggling to stand. Then his leg buckled and he almost toppled over. Meanwhile, the audiovisual system still blared.

Realizing he was all but finished, Eight Two glanced at the instructor. He looked on impassively.

She stepped forward and offered Tree her hand. He shot her a dazed look and for a second she thought she recognized a glimmer of humanity in them. Taking her hand, he clambered back to his feet.

She almost slipped the elbow strike, but was a split-second slow. The point of Tree's elbow smashed into the edge of her jaw and everything went black.

Doctor Marnisha Copeland glanced out the window of the X22 vertjet as it banked hard out of the clouds. From thousands of feet above, the ground was nothing but a giant swathe of yellow desert. As the aircraft continued its turn she made out the ruins of a city and spotted what remained of the central business district. The hulking shells of tall skyscrapers jutted from the sand like fossilized trunks of an ancient forest.

The Sakkin scientist had visited the former capital of Jordan before the Greater Middle Eastern Conflict. Back then it had been a bustling modern city with a population of three million. Unfortunately for them their government had thrown its hand in with the Caliphate. The armed forces of Israel had wiped them from the face of the earth. Now all that remained of the once proud city of Amman were ruins being slowly devoured by the desert.

A soft whine filled the cabin and she felt the jet slow, beginning its transition from horizontal flight to landing mode.

"Ma'am, we will arrive in four minutes," the autonomous flight system announced in a flat voice.

Marnisha yawned as she raised the back of her chair. It was a six-hour flight from Sakkin's headquarters in Cape Town to the facility in Amman, a trip she was forced to take every month to evaluate trainee development. Stretching her neck she slipped a compact flexipad from the pocket of her two-piece suit and held it in front of her face. "Mirror," she said.

The transparent device immediately displayed her facial features. She studied the image, paying particular attention to her lipstick and eyeliner. Despite being sixty-five years old she did not look a day over thirty. Her long auburn hair was devoid of gray and her elfin features unblemished by age. Genetic manipulation had slowed the physical decline of her cells to less than a third of the speed nature intended. At that rate she would not resemble her actual age until she was well past a hundred. She sighed, taking a makeup kit from her bag. Despite the advances in genetic manipulation, women still resorted to painting themselves to accent their features.

Touching up her face she registered the change in speed as the vertjet slowed dramatically and landed with a soft thud. Checking the window she watched as the landing pad descended and the city ruins disappeared, replaced by reinforced concrete.

She rose from her leather chair, smoothed her skirt and retrieved a jacket from an overhead locker. Donning it she walked along the aisle to the ramp at the rear. It dropped with a hiss and she strode down it in high heels. Glancing up she caught a brief glimpse of a dusty orange sky as, far above her head, the hangar roof closed.

Sakkin's agent training facility, the *Institute*, was buried hundreds of feet below the abandoned city. The Middle East was now a wasteland, referred to as the morass. A hostile environment, it was home to nomadic tribes and bands of survivors attempting to scrape a livelihood from the ruins. It was the perfect location for a deniable facility that none of the countries of the Advanced Block (ADBLOK) wanted inside their highly secure, and civilized, borders.

She walked between a pair of militarized variants of the X22 to the hangar door where two figures dressed in black

Sakkin uniforms waited. As she got closer she identified the facility's head trainer, Leon Wilken, and chief psychologist, Shona Demski.

Leon was somewhat of a legend within Sakkin Industries. The former Israeli Sayeret Matkal operative had fought in every major conflict since the war on the Islamic State in 2014. He was a master of combat, subterfuge and deniable operations. Short with a compact and powerful frame Leon was handsome with a jutting chin, strong nose and piercing blue eyes. On face value Marnisha put his age at around forty. However, she knew he was nearly eighty. She also knew that he was sleeping with the woman who stood beside him.

Shona Demski was the facility's resident psychologist, responsible for the mental development and stability of the trainees. Like Leon, she was short, however where he was muscular and combat hardened she was curvaceous. A dirty blonde with doe-like eyes, her very presence annoyed Marnisha.

Both employees wore the standard Sakkin uniform; black combat shirts, pants and boots. Leon wore a utility belt lined with pouches and a pistol on his right hip.

"Doctor Copeland, welcome back to the *Institute*," he said warmly as he took her hand.

"Hello, Leon," she said, ignoring Shona.

She caught the scowl on the other woman's face as Leon directed her out of the hangar.

"Did you see the intelligence update this morning?" he asked.

"No, I didn't get a chance to read it before I left Cape Town."

"One of our security teams in the Congo was attacked.

Four mechops destroyed and two of my graduates seriously wounded." His eyes narrowed. "We're not dealing with rag-tag fighters. The CEO believes this to be the work of professionals."

"The intensity of these attacks seems to be increasing. Perhaps you should reevaluate your methods of dealing with the indigenous elements."

He snorted. "Eradication is the only course of action. Hearts and minds is a failed concept. Empathy is a weakness that cost us our homeland."

She ignored the comment as they entered the facility's armory. They passed rows of lockers containing body armor, hulking black exoskeleton suits and racks of weapons. It was where the *Institute's* students geared up before conducting their training.

As they waited for the elevator she turned and glanced into a workshop bay. An elderly dark-skinned man in a wheelchair was working on a mechop, one of the robotic warriors Sakkin used to augment their ground forces. Nicknamed 'clankers' they were only capable of following simple directions and wielding firepower. Compared to her operatives they were blunt killing instruments.

The technician turned to her with sad eyes and she studied his weathered features. "Who is that?"

Leon shot him a glance as the elevator arrived. "That's our weapons tech. Keeps everything running."

They entered the high-speed elevator and Shona positioned herself between the two.

"Why is he in a wheelchair?"

"His legs are useless," replied Leon as he selected a floor and the elevator rose. "He doesn't need them to work, so they haven't been replaced."

She nodded as they reached their level. Simple economics, she could not argue with that. The doors opened revealing a semi-circle room with wall-to-wall screens. Inside half a dozen staff sat behind curved touch screens, fixated on the information displayed before them.

This was the *Institute's* operations room. From here Leon and his team monitored and controlled almost every aspect of the training environment and the trainees. They could access individual data that included vital signs, brain activity and even blood chemistry. With this information they would customize the training scenarios to challenge the students.

She followed Leon across the floor to the curved wall. As they approached, a panel slid into the ceiling and he led them into a smaller room with a conference table and chairs. He sat at the head of the table with Marnisha to his right. Once Shona entered the panel locked back in place, isolating them from the operations room.

Leon pushed a flexipad across the table to her. "Do you want to discuss all of the trainees or go straight to the problem?"

She arched an eyebrow. "Problem?"

"Yes, we've had significant issues with Eight Two," said Shona.

"What kind of problems?"

"She's failing her training," said Leon. "System, show me trainee Eight Two's evaluation stats."

She turned her head so she could see the glass walls as they displayed a series of bar graphs with symbols next to them. Interpreting the information, she frowned. "These indicate she is passing in all areas except psyche and unarmed combat."

"Correct," Shona said. "However, it is my opinion that she has significant psychological flaws that render her ineffective as a Sakkin operative, in particular, her empathy levels." She rose and gestured to one of the bars on the screen. The graphic enlarged, splitting into different psychological attributes that included: perception, reasoning, problem solving, adaptability, empathy, obedience and discipline.

Marnisha drummed her fingers on the glass table as she analyzed the information.

"There was an incident this morning, during an unarmed combat session," added Leon. "System, recall the knockout sequence from Eight Two's fight."

A freeze frame of the unarmed combat facility appeared on the walls. Trainee Eight Two was standing over a dazed male opponent.

"At this point, she had successfully evaded neutralization and was poised for a dispatch strike. However, it didn't pan out that way," said Leon. "Play sequence."

The clip advanced and she watched as the female trainee stepped forward and offered her hand. As she pulled the downed trainee to his feet the video slowed. She grimaced as the larger trainee drove his elbow into the jaw of Eight Two, smashing the lower mandible from her face. The teenager collapsed to the mat like a rag doll.

Leon and Shona remained silent.

"Where is she now?" she asked.

"System, show trainee Eight Two."

The screen changed to a high-resolution shot of the facility's infirmary. Eight Two lay on a sleek white gurney with medical robots and sensors clustered around her body. Marnisha could see the devastating damage to her jaw. It hung from her face like a mangled pork chop.

"Why hasn't she been repaired?"

Shona pursed her lips. "We believe that would be a

waste of resources. She lacks the ruthlessness to be successful. The logical option is termination."

Marnisha shook her head slowly then turned and stared at the psychologist. "Get out."

Shona reacted with a surprised look. "It is my job to evaluate every trainee." She turned to Leon.

He gestured to the door and it hissed open.

She huffed and stormed out, the door closing behind her.

"Leon, need I remind you who runs this project."

"The girl is a liability. She—"

"Will be returned to training, immediately."

His jaw bulged as he clenched his teeth. "Why is she so important?"

"Because Sakkin Industries has invested significant resources into her development. It is your job to equip her with the skills to survive in the morass."

He gestured to the image being beamed from the infirmary. "Survive? She won't survive the *Tsalmaveth*, let alone out there. She's a waste of resources that could be allocated to another potential operative."

Marnisha was familiar with the *Institute's* training program. She knew the *Tsalmaveth*, or Shadow of Death, was the final combat phase. It was a brutal week of testing that involved live targets, live fire and death to those who couldn't make the grade. She reached into her bag and removed a nano drive. "Train her Leon. Because, if you don't I'll have your little toy transferred to another facility." She slid the drive across the table. "I want you to replace the final simulated training session with this."

He scowled as he picked up the device. "What is it?"

"Something unique." She rose from her seat. "I'll be in the lab reviewing the other trainees."

"What's so special about this girl?"

She arched one of her perfectly sculpted eyebrows. "Make sure your 'toy' isn't around for our next meeting. Her stupidity offends me." With that, she turned and walked out of the room, leaving Leon sitting with the drive in his hand.

Chapter Three

The Institute, Jordan

Eight Two's eyes flashed open and she sat upright, clutching at her face. The last thing she remembered was Tree's elbow smashing into her jaw.

Her fingers delicately probed her jawline, but there was no sign of bruising much less the break she expected to find. She glanced around and realized that she was in the *Institute's* medical bay. It was a place all the trainees were familiar with. Injuries were frequent and the advanced medical technologies ensured they were kept fighting fit.

An itching sensation told her that the injury had been repaired using synthetic flesh. She'd experienced it once before, when her arm was burnt during weapons training.

"Eight Two, your injury has been repaired. You will now report to the immersion facility," announced a bland female voice from a speaker overhead.

She swung her legs off the padded bed and left the surgical bay through a sliding door. A med tech sitting behind a bank of screens gave her a nod as she exited the infirmary into a sterile corridor.

Unaffected by the surgery she strode purposefully to the central elevators. A breakthrough in medical technology had long since negated the need for sedatives and their side effects.

As she rode the elevator to the immersion facility she relived the moments before the elbow strike that had knocked her unconscious and shattered her jaw. She had offered Tree her help but he'd exploited it. He identified her kindness as a weakness and used it for his own benefit. Her jaw twinged and she realized it was clenched along with her fists.

Exhaling she stepped out of the elevator and drove the aggression from her body. Kindness was a weakness and like rage it could be controlled. The next time the opportunity presented to destroy one of her classmates she would seize it with both hands.

The rest of her squad was already locked in their immersion pods when she entered the facility. She found an empty one and climbed in, lowering the lid.

Resembling giant bean-shaped coffins the pods were padded inside and climate controlled. She nestled into the memory foam bed and closed her eyes.

Instantly she was transported into the familiar world of the Sakkin Industries virtual immersion training environment, interfacing with her nervous system via a chip embedded at the base of her skull.

"Welcome, trainee Eight Two," announced a female narrator. "This lesson will commence with a recap of the historical events leading up to the Greater Middle Eastern Conflict of 2045."

Eight Two rolled her eyes. Every history lesson started

with a recap, summarizing the previous lesson. It felt like Sakkin was bashing their version of the events down her throat at every opportunity. She exhaled and readied herself for the experience.

Suddenly she found herself floating over a sandy desert marked with burning villages.

"In the year 2025 Chinese-backed mercenaries commenced operations in the disputed Lake Chad zone against Cameroonian nationals," narrated the female voice. "Led by Nigerian officers, they argued that they were was securing vital water supplies being squandered by Cameroon. French Special Forces supported by Ice Hand Private Military Contractors and Cameroon Army units deployed into the area and conflict escalated. By early 2026 the disagreement had claimed close to ten thousand lives."

Eight Two found herself on the ground moving through devastated villages. Bodies littered the ground and the stench of burning flesh filled her nose. "It's only a simulation," she reminded herself.

"By mid-2026 following demands for French and PMC forces to withdraw, China moved their newly commissioned aircraft carrier into the Gulf of Guinea. In a short space of time Chinese aircraft commenced flying in support of ground troops."

Her view changed to a large map with three-dimensional ships and aircraft moving over it.

"The French responded with their own carrier and in December a Chinese MiG shot down a French Rafale in Cameroon airspace. The French retaliated by sinking a Chinese frigate."

She watched as the tiny aircraft and ships attacked each other.

"The situation escalated further when a Chinese submarine torpedoed the French Carrier Charles de Gaulle causing significant damage. The Chinese government subsequently demanded the withdrawal of all French forces from the Chad Lake area. On 17 November 2026 the Chinese carrier Liaoning was torpedoed and sunk by an unknown submarine."

Eight Two felt a resounding sadness as the narrative continued. She'd heard it all before, this was the beginning of the end of the modern world. China retaliated against the US by targeting all of their space-based assets and sowing orbit with antisatellite mines. The United State's response had been even more devastating. They defaulted on their debt repayments and isolated China from the markets she relied on for economic survival. By the 2030s the country had imploded. The PLA disintegrated and the once proud People's Republic of China splintered into hundreds of tribal fiefdoms ruled by generals and warlords.

She watched as a map of the world appeared and flaming hot spots flared covering the globe. Nations fell and tens of thousands of people died. The next information sequences were the ones she dreaded the most. A knot formed in her stomach as the narrative continued.

"In 2034 a plague pandemic swept the globe."

Now she was on the ground in a refugee camp in South East Asia. Everywhere she turned there were sick and dying people. She watched helplessly as a woman sat clutching a dead child, rocking as she wailed.

"It is estimated that between twenty-five and thirty percent of the population of the developing world succumbed to the virus. Losses in the first world were significantly lower, limited to the weak and elderly."

Eight Two was transported from a slum in Asia to the corridors of a modern hospital. It was a different story here.

The medical staff moved with efficiency and there was hope on the faces of those waiting to see loved ones. This was the difference between the two worlds, the difference between the haves and the have-nots.

"In 2036 a firm in California, Sumsunto, revolutionized clean energy with their miniature cold fusion technology. Within a year of this revelation The Republic of California seceded from the United States."

The map reappeared and a tear ran from her eye.

"With the United States dissolved, opportunist radical elements in the Middle East toppled the remnants of the Syrian and Iraqi governments forming a powerful Caliphate. This organization immediately commenced a campaign of terrorism designed to cripple the Jewish people's will to fight. It was in this environment that Sakkin Industries came to the fore as Israel's most powerful weapon against the Caliphate. In a global environment of terror and unrest Sakkin enabled the civilized world to protect itself from harm."

Making it the most divisive organization in the history of the world, she thought. The Caliphate's campaign had played directly into the hands of the powerful corporation. Sakkin sold the wealthiest countries the means to close their borders and isolate themselves, and their wealth, from the rest of the global population. The rich hid behind their walls protected by drones, clankers and security operatives.

She'd come from beyond those walls. Sakkin operatives had rescued her from certain death at the hands of marauders and for that she was grateful. However, that didn't stop her from feeling for those not born into the wealth of the ADBLOK. Her people were from outside and she felt a longing to be with them. Something told her she did not belong among the ranks of Sakkin's orphan assassins.

"In 2042 the Caliphate's war of terrorism came to a bloody conclusion," continued the narrator. "Jordan, having recently joined the axis of evil, was able to construct a small and primitive nuclear device. The weapon was infiltrated through the Palestinian territories, finally detected by Sakkin operatives at a crossing point into Jerusalem. Upon discovery it was detonated destroying the city and vaporizing nearly thirty thousand residents."

Eight Two stood at the checkpoint as the device detonated. She felt the heat as a wave of energy swept across the city, pulverizing it. Despite knowing that everything was a high-tech simulation, she still felt the icy grip of fear. People exploded into flaming torches as the narrator continued weaving her story of death and destruction.

Then suddenly, Eight Two found herself standing in a sleek white equipment hangar with the rest of squad *Gurion*. She locked eyes with the three-dimensional render of Tree and held his steely gaze. A smirk crept onto his face and then he looked away.

"Today's lesson covers the tactics employed by Sakkin operatives in the immediate aftermath of the Caliphate attack on Jerusalem," announced the narrator as the rear doors of the hangar opened, revealing a bustling operations room. "You will travel with the operatives as they identify and prosecute targets linked to the attack."

Eight Two followed the rest of the squad through the doors into the operations room as they listened to the history of Operation Retribution. However, her thoughts weren't on the lesson, she was staring at the back of Tree's head and planning how she was going to make him pay.

There was a combat training mission scheduled for the next period. That might provide the opportunity she needed.

Two hours later, in one of the *Institute's* briefing rooms, a black-uniformed Sakkin instructor stood over a holographic projector. Squad *Gurion* was arrayed in a semi-circle before him.

"The target for this mission is an isolated village on the outskirts of the city. Terrorist elements are using it as a staging base to attack a nearby mining camp. Your mission is to eliminate all hostiles and secure the target compound."

Eight Two studied the 3D image intently as he spoke. The village was not one she was familiar with. It consisted of densely packed mud buildings that increased in size toward the middle of the settlement. A single lane road ran from the outskirts to a central two-story residence, the target compound.

"How many hostiles?" asked one of her teammates.

"Intel estimates upwards of twenty."

"Weapons?" Eight Two asked.

"The usual legacy small arms, maybe some rockets and mortars. No indication of modern weaponry."

Tree smirked at her. "Better look out though, they've probably got elbows."

The others snickered.

"Oh, so you're going to let the women beat you out there too?" she fired back.

The instructor snorted. "OK, cut the shit talking. Three Three, you're the ground commander. How are you going to tackle this?"

Tree glared at her then dropped his eyes to the map.

"We'll make the drop a half mile short of the town. Five Seven, you and Three Four have the right flank. Five Five and I will take a left." He turned his attention to Eight Two. "You can take the center line with the clankers."

She shrugged. "No problem."

The instructor nodded. "Right then, we're wheels up at landing pad three in fifteen minutes. Move to your allocated suits and make sure your gear is good to go."

The equipment they needed was stored in the central armory one floor below the briefing facility. They rode the elevator in silence before heading to their lockers. Eight Two grabbed her full-face combat helmet and slipped a set of lightweight underarmor over her torso. Then she strapped a graphene laminate combat knife to the inside of her forearm.

She moved to the bays where the berserker suits and mechops were kept. When she arrived at her allocated suit she found a wheelchair-bound weapons technician running a diagnostic.

"Hello," she said.

He looked up with a startled expression. "I'm sorry, ma'am. I thought I had a few more minutes to finish up."

"It's OK, I can wait. We're a little early."

He nodded and turned back to the flexipad he had plugged into the suit.

Eight Two stepped forward and watched over his shoulder. The man's fingers flashed across the screen, checking each of the suit's systems. "So you're the one who fixes everything we break?"

He backed his wheelchair out of the bay. "Yes, ma'am."

She shot him a broad smile. "Thank you. Your hard work is appreciated."

The man returned a curious look as he nodded slowly. "My pleasure."

Eight Two watched as he pushed his wheelchair toward the workshop. She had seen him before but never had the opportunity to talk to him. He had a kind face with sad eyes that reminded her of a basset hound.

"Get a move on!" bellowed Tree. "We launch in ten."

She shot him a withering glare as she activated her berserker suit. The exoskeleton's frontal armor peeled open, revealing the padded interior cockpit. Climbing inside she gave the suit a moment to adjust to her predetermined settings. Then she slipped her hands into the gauntlets and closed up.

She exhaled slowly as the plates locked in place and the system slaved to her helmet. This was what Sakkin called a berserker suit. Fully enclosed it was designed to protect operatives from all but the heaviest of weapons. Eight Two found it a little claustrophobic. She preferred the lightweight jumper suits they wore for air insertion missions.

The transparent shield in front of her eyes came alive, displaying information from the suit's sensors. Symbols lit up at the edges of her vision, telling her that all functions were online and operable. She stepped out of the bay and clunked her way along the aisle. No matter how many times she wore the suit it was still alien. It felt like she was wading through thick mud as she maneuvered it to where the mechops hung suspended from a rack.

Mechanical Operatives or mechops were the backbone of Sakkin's security forces. Roughly humanoid in size and shape they had a cluster of sensors where their heads should be and a matte gray finish that changed color depending on their surroundings.

The trainees called them clankers, due to their limited

artificial intelligence and the sound they made when they moved. Capable of completing basic tasks they were directed by either voice commands or through a berserker suit interface.

Her clankers hung on the same rack, each marked with a flashing green light. She activated them, slaving them to her suit's battle management system. When they were online the rack turned, depositing them on the ground where they stood tall and strode across to join her.

Her suit and the clankers were armed with a variety of weapons. She had a lightweight railer affixed to one arm, a plasma rocket launcher tucked over her shoulder and various non-lethal systems hidden behind armored covers. The clankers carried heavier railers with an assortment of projectiles, including high explosive, armor piercing and plasma.

With her clankers in tow, she left the armory. As she entered the cavernous hangar she noticed a sleek corporate X22 parked on the central pad. Someone important must be visiting, she thought.

She rounded the jet and spotted her team waiting behind their allocated craft, a boxier military grade MX22. Her brow furrowed as she saw a second figure, dressed in fatigues, standing with their instructor. As she got closer she identified him as the senior from the dining hall, Seven Nine Nine.

She stopped at the rear of the group with the clankers behind her.

"Team," announced the instructor. "This is senior trainee Seven Nine Nine. He will be observing this mission to familiarize himself with your strengths and weaknesses. In the next phase of training he will be commanding squad *Gurion*."

Eight Two glanced at Seven Nine Nine and found him staring directly at her. She met his steely gaze with one of her own, through the helmet. Probably saw her as the weak point of the team, she thought. Well, he was about to find out how wrong that assumption was.

"Right then," said the instructor. "Mount up."

The scream of the MX22's engines filled the hold as it decelerated and flared. Eight Two felt her stomach lurch as they came to a hover and the ramp lowered. The other trainees jumped first. Eight Two and her clankers followed close behind. She passed the instructor and Seven Nine Nine, both remained strapped into their seats wearing virtual reality headsets. They would be watching her every move, looking for weakness. She ignored them and leaped clear of the vertjet.

The fifteen-yard drop would have shattered the legs of any normal human being. Encased in her suit of powered berserker armor Eight Two was anything but normal. She executed a classic superhero crouch as she impacted. Her clankers slammed down either side.

The MX22's thrusters whipped the sand and dust around her into a violent maelstrom as it rocketed skyward. She strode through the sandstorm and reviewed her surroundings.

Flashing markers projected on the inside of her helmet showed her where the other trainees were on the bleak landscape. Their suits, like hers and the clankers, had matched their adaptive camouflage to the surroundings, making them difficult to see with the naked eye.

"Eight Two, get a move on," ordered Tree over their

communications link. He and the others were sprinting across the desert to their positions.

A scowl made its way to her face as she broke into a run. There was no need for the order; they all knew their role in the attack. "Mechops adopt two up formation, maintain twenty-yard spacing," she commanded her clankers.

A vast swath of wasteland surrounded the abandoned desert village. Her carbon fiber boots crunched over what was once fertile land. It had been laid bare by Israel's weapons of mass destruction. Her suit's life support sensors told her the outside temperature was 108 degrees. Despite the intense heat she felt no discomfort as she ran at thirty miles an hour. The suit's cooling system kept her body at an optimum operating temperature.

She slowed a half-mile from the outskirts of the village, allowing the clankers to scout forward. Tree had launched two hunter drones. The disc-shaped craft were hovering over the town. As yet their sensors had not detected any hostiles.

Her heart rate increased slightly in anticipation of contact. It might be a training mission, but that didn't mean the hostiles wouldn't be shooting back. The *Institute* didn't believe in a softly-softly approach to training. The clankers that replicated the enemy were armed with the same weapons they could expect to find in the hands of hostiles in the morass.

As her mechops reached the edge of the village they reported movement. Red hostile indicators appeared on her heads-up display, and the drones moved to investigate. Bringing up the battle map on the HUD she saw that the symbols were close to the center, within a short distance of the main target compound. She instructed the clankers forward along the main thoroughfare. Following, she kept to one side of the building-lined street.

The houses on the outskirts were little more than mud-brick huts. She activated her railer when she spotted fresh bullet holes in a burnt out car. Shiny steel glinted in the harsh midday sun as she paused in an empty doorway.

"Eight Two, push your damn clankers forward, or this is going to take all day," ordered Tree.

Checking the digital map again, she confirmed his location. He was skirting the village, well clear of the identified hostiles. She had a curt response on her tongue but chose to ignore him instead.

Ahead her clankers were advancing slowly along the street, their weapons held ready. As she stepped out from behind a building there was an almighty explosion and a burnt car flipped into the air. Shrapnel and stones pinged off her armor as she dashed for the cover of a bullet-ridden wall.

The high-pitched snap of a railer penetrator told her the clankers were returning fire. Heart racing she held her railer over the wall and zoomed the optics.

Her mouth went dry as she spotted the barrel of a tank poking from inside a walled compound. The antiquated war machine belched flame and a clanker was thrown through the air. It landed a short distance from her in a smoking shattered mess of cables and hydraulics.

"What the hell is going on over there?" demanded Tree.

"They said there were no heavy weapons!" she screamed.

There was a pause. "The situation has changed. Deal with it."

She shook her head and mumbled, "Great leadership."

Another explosion shook the ground as the tank fired. If

she didn't move fast it was going to destroy her last clanker, or worse.

"Do you need support?" asked Tree.

"No. I'm dealing with it."

She issued verbal commands to her remaining clanker. It immediately fired off a volley of smoke grenades that filled the street with dense gray smoke.

The tank could have a thermal imager, but it wouldn't help. Both the clanker and her exoskeleton emitted the same signature as the terrain around them. She activated a harassment order for the clanker before sprinting across the street and bounding onto the roof of an adjacent building.

She leaped from rooftop to rooftop, advancing toward the target compound and the tank. Bullets cracked through the air as other hostiles spotted her. Her helmet marked the attackers with red indicators. On the move she returned fire.

Her railer launched hypervelocity tungsten penetrators at four times the speed of sound. They hit their target with devastating lethality tearing through walls and blowing apart an enemy clanker.

She reached the rooftop under which the tank was hiding. It fired again, aiming for her remaining clanker. Her HUD indicated he was still active. As she drew a demolition charge from her suit she found herself wondering why the clankers were referred to as 'he.' Her eyes narrowed as she placed the charge on the roof. Maybe if they made them women they wouldn't be so stupid.

Rolling sideways she activated the charge. The building shook as it smashed a hole through the reinforced concrete exposing the turret of the tank. She dropped through the smoke and dust and landed on top with a clang. Her gauntlets grasped the hatch and she tore it off.

The tank's engine roared and it lurched forward,

smashing through a wall. Eight Two clung to the turret as bricks and beams rained down on her. Then, as the armored vehicle rumbled out onto the street she dropped a plasma grenade inside. The charge detonated as she leaped clear.

A column of molten plasma erupted from the turret. The tank ground to a halt, fire spewing from every opening.

"Tank destroyed. Moving on to primary target," she reported as she strode away from the blazing wreck. Smoke billowed across the village as her remaining clanker appeared and fell in alongside.

Adrenalin coursed through her body as she stormed along the street. Targets appeared in doorways and windows but she left them for the clanker to eliminate as she sprinted for the central compound.

A pair of heavy wooden doors disintegrated as she punched her way through them. Heart pumping she barged into a central courtyard with her railer held ready.

She paused and for a split second could almost hear the voices of the family who would have occupied the once opulent residence. Now the central pond and fountain were dry and the tiled floor covered in sand. A rustle from the upper level reached her ears and she turned to the possible threat. When nothing appeared she scanned the room, searching for the staircase. It was located in the far corner. She kept her weapon aimed high as she made her way toward it.

Gunfire echoed through the courtyard as she climbed the stairs. Bullets stitched the mud walls around her. She ducked behind a pillar and returned fire. Her clanker appeared and she ordered him to provide covering fire as she stormed the next level.

As she reached the landing she spotted two mechops

armed with assault rifles. Her railer snapped twice, blasting them off their feet.

She moved from room to room, destroying another three targets. With the upper level cleared she rejoined her clanker on the ground floor.

"Eight Two, what's your status?" demanded Tree.

"Target compound will be cleared imminently," she replied as she moved to another room. As she scanned an abandoned kitchen it dawned on her that the village wasn't unlike the one from her dreams. The shacks on the outskirts were made from the same materials, mud-brick and tin sheeting. For a split second she felt a glimmer of recognition. Then she remembered the river and the marketplace, this town had neither.

As she made to leave she heard a noise from the corner of the room. Turning to investigate she dialed up the helmet's laser microphone. The sensitive beam amplified what sounded like a rat scuffling under the floor. Then, she heard a faint whimper.

Crouching she spotted a wooden hatch under a thick coating of sand. Hooking a mechanical finger under it she aimed her railer with the other hand and heaved it up. Her thermal vision automatically activated, revealing a narrow well-worn set of stairs.

She thought she heard another whimper. There was no way she could fit down the stairs while wearing the berserker suit. She considered sending the clanker, but it would not fit either.

"Eight Two, confirm target building is secure," transmitted Tree.

"Target secure. All hostiles eliminated." She brought up the battle map and could see that the rest of the squad had cleared their sectors.

There was a pause and then the instructor's voice replaced Tree's. "Mission is complete, move to landing point Alpha for extraction."

She stared into the cellar and found herself wondering who was hiding below. Was it someone like her? Someone who had managed to escape from the bandits and murderers who roamed the morass? She shut down her suit killing the data signal.

"Eight Two, is something wrong?" asked the instructor over the emergency frequency.

She activated the release on the exoskeleton and stepped out. "I've got a minor problem with my suit. I'm going to run a full reboot." She unsnapped an emergency pistol from the leg of the suit and slipped into the narrow space.

As she moved slowly down the dust-covered stairs she was acutely aware of how vulnerable she was without the exoskeleton. Her helmet and underarmor would only stop a small caliber bullet.

Her heart pounded as she scanned the room over the barrel of her pistol. She spotted two glowing figures huddled in the corner of the chamber, children. She stood perfectly still, not wanting to alarm them. As she was about to speak Tree's voice sounded, "Eight Two confirm you have identified two hostiles in your location."

"Negative, my suit's rebooting then I'll move to the extraction point."

There was a pause and another voice replaced Tree's. "Neutralize the targets and then move out." It was Seven Nine Nine, the senior who would be taking over as squad leader.

"There are no targets in my location. I repeat there are no targets here."

There was a pause. "Your sensors may be impacted. I am sending another operative to investigate."

She turned and dashed up the stairs, leaving the children behind. Climbing through the trap door, she slammed it shut, kicked sand across it and turned back to her exoskeleton. As she did Tree stomped into the room and fixed her with a glare.

"Where are the hostiles?"

She shrugged, stepped into her suit and activated it. The armor plates snapped into place around her. "My sensors were playing up."

His eyes narrowed behind his faceplate. "Yeah, right. Well, you already screwed the assault by getting your clanker trashed."

She returned the steely gaze. "The mission was a success and no one told us about the tank."

"Whatever, let's see what the evaluation says. Now get to the extraction point, pickup is two minutes out."

She walked out of the room and into the courtyard, then glanced over her shoulder. Tree wasn't following. She waited a full twenty seconds before he appeared.

"Get a hustle on," he said as he strode past.

The two operatives and the remaining clanker left the building and started along the street. As they reached the burning tank, there was an explosion behind them. Eight Two's heart stopped as she spun and watched a ball of flame roll into the air above the target compound.

"Turns out there were rats in the cellar."

Tears streamed down her cheeks as oily black smoke rolled into the blue sky. Grief turned to rage and she imagined lifting her railer and firing a tungsten penetrator directly through Tree's face. Turning from the funeral pyre she ran toward the extraction zone.

Minutes later, she sat in the hold of the MX22 as it rocketed over the desert below. Her teammates sat calmly in their suits while the instructor and senior trainee reviewed the mission at their workstations. The craft rocked as they hit turbulence, shaking a tear loose from the corner of her eye.

Despite the presence of the others she had never felt more alone. She had nothing in common with those around her. Tree had murdered innocent children without the slightest hint of remorse. He was an ice-cold killer, they all were. She glanced at the mechanical hands of the berserker suit and realized that she was becoming the same. Sakkin was not offering orphaned refugees a second chance, they were turning them into murderers.

Chapter Four

The Institute, Jordan

Eight Two fought back tears as she deactivated the berserker suit inside its bay and stepped out. As she removed her helmet she found herself staring at the hard features of Seven Nine Nine.

"Your move on the tank was text book," the senior trainee admitted.

She managed a nod as his gray eyes bored into hers.

"But, Three Three identified two targets that you missed."

"There was a problem with my suit. The power levels slumped reducing the sensor range."

His eyes narrowed. "So you didn't know they were there?"

"No, otherwise I would have neutralized them."

"Of course." He stared a moment longer before the arrival of the wheelchair-bound technician drew his attention. "This suit has a defect," he snarled. "It failed at a critical point and could have cost this operative her life."

The technician's brow furrowed. "I don't understand." He looked to Eight Two. "I ran a full diagnostic immediately before you left."

"You don't understand? Well that's the problem, isn't it? Perhaps I should report you to the staff. I'm sure they wouldn't tolerate your incompetence."

Eight Two bit her tongue.

"Sir, I can run another check," said the technician.

"So I'm a liar?" hissed Seven Nine Nine.

The man shook his head. "No, sir."

"Then you failed to correctly execute your responsibilities."

Eight Two's face burned with the shame of her lie. "The fault may have occurred as a result of my attack on the tank."

The senior trainee's steely gaze returned to her. "That's unlikely. The RX304 is particularly robust."

The old man shook his head in disagreement. "A significant explosive concussion—"

Seven Nine Nine pounced, grabbing the crippled man's throat. "I don't want to hear your excuses."

"It's not his fault," she snapped, slipping the combat knife from her forearm. "Release him."

The edge of the black blade gleamed menacingly.

The technician gasped as Seven Nine Nine released his throat. "Is that a threat?"

She spun the knife in her palm, over the back of her hand and returned it to the scabbard. "No, it's a request."

He stared at her for a moment longer then turned on his heel and stormed away. Eight Two exhaled as she watched him disappear.

"Thank you," said the technician.

She turned to him and managed a slight nod. In her mind, she was imagining the ways the new squad leader was going to make her life hell. She may have just made the worst decision of her life.

"You're not like the others," said the man as he offered her his hand. "My name is Henry."

She shook his hand. "I'm Eight Two."

He frowned. "You don't have real names?"

"No, only the numbers."

"We had numbers when I was in the Corps."

"The Corps?"

"The US Marine Corps." He registered her blank expression. "Never mind. Let's check out this suit of yours." He produced a flexipad.

"There's no problem with the sensors," she said.

He looked up with a frown. "What do you mean?"

She sighed. "I made it up."

"Why would you do that?"

"So I wouldn't have to kill two children."

Henry's eyes went wide before he shook his head and turned back to the flexipad. "Well, it turns out the ultracapacitor isn't holding a charge. The output is fluctuating dramatically. That would have a significant impact on its capability. I'll make sure it's logged." He rolled in behind the exoskeleton. There was a click followed by a hiss of gas and he reappeared holding a cylinder the size of a flashlight.

"That's the ultracapacitor?" she asked.

He placed it on his lap. "Yeah, this little sucker holds enough power to run a small village." Wheeling his way out of the bay, he stopped in front of Eight Two and studied her face. "Nope, you're definitely not like the others.

She stared into his bloodshot eyes and reached out, placing her hand on his shoulder. "Thank you for covering for me."

He smiled broadly. "That's what friends do."

The comment caught her by surprise. She had not heard the word friend in a long time much less actually had one. In fact, the last friend she could remember was the boy who had died in her dreams.

A series of beeps emitted from her watch reminding her she had a mission debriefing to attend. "I have to go. But, I hope I'll see you soon, Henry."

As she walked out of the armory toward the elevators she felt something she had not experienced in a very long time, belonging.

Eight Two lay on her bed staring at the ceiling. She was exhausted, but sleep would not come easy. Every time she closed her eyes she saw the two children huddled in the corner of the room. A moment later fire would sweep through the cellar engulfing them. As they writhed in agony, she'd see their faces. One was hers and the other a face from her dreams, the boy who'd tried to save her in the village attack, her friend.

She'd shed tears for them, cried until her eyes were red and the collar of her uniform wet. But no amount of tears would bring them back and no amount of crying could ease the feeling of loneliness that overwhelmed her.

Sitting up she wiped her face and reached for the flexipad on her desk. The opaque plastic came alive with color as her fingers touched it. She navigated the menus with deft strokes, bypassing the Sakkin training interface to get to the underlying operating system.

When she had arrived at the Institute it had taken her less than a week to work out how to access the facility's maintenance and systems data. While that didn't let her into the Sakkin training servers, it did allow her to examine the layout of the facility. Of particular interest was the sprawling ventilation system that filtered air from the surface and distributed it throughout the underground complex.

She traced a route through the ducts from her room to the hangar and armory level. It was two floors above. She committed the path to memory as she checked for cameras and sensors. The *Institute* was riddled with them, except for the ventilation system and the trainee's rooms. That made sense. Sleep and internal security weren't a priority at the *Institute*. All they cared about were the training facilities and how well their mindless killers were performing.

Climbing onto her desk she popped the ceiling panel where she hid her notebook. Behind it was a ventilation shaft. It took her a moment to unclip the grill and reveal the ducting that carried fresh air.

Pulling herself up into the gap she slid feet first into the narrow pipe. Then she reached behind her head and slotted the ceiling panel back in place. Sliding feet first she reached a junction where she turned so she could crawl.

The inside of the pipe was smooth, making progress swift. She slid through the darkness, mentally tracking her progress. Ignoring the offshoots that led to the other trainee's rooms she moved along the central line.

In a few short minutes she reached a vertical shaft. Wedging herself into the conduit she used the grip of her combat trainers to propel herself, inch by inch, up to the next level. Despite the climate controlled air she was sweating when she reached the lip and pulled herself into the next horizontal tube. She checked her watch. It was a little after 2200 hours. She'd been crawling for less than fifteen minutes.

It took another five to reach her target vent. Popping the grill she stuck her head out into the bright lighting of the workshop. Scanning the room she confirmed there was no one around.

Having successfully reached her destination she now faced the challenge of dropping from the vent. The wall opposite was lined with shelving. It was a little over two yards away. If she jumped, there was a good chance she could reach it.

"You're going to hurt yourself." The voice came from directly below.

She glanced down and saw Henry, looking up.

"I'll send the robot up."

She watched as he worked his flexipad.

There was a whine from the corner of the room and an electric cart with a folding hydraulic arm appeared. It parked below and the arm extended toward her. "Will it hold my weight?"

"It lifts far heavier than you, little lady."

She reached out and grasped the robotic claw, then swung out and wrapped her legs around the arm. It lowered to the ground and she dropped onto the smooth floor.

"Doing a little duct maintenance?" quipped Henry as she rose.

She managed a smile. "I thought I'd drop in on a friend."

He grinned. "Well, I'd better show you around then." He pushed his wheelchair across the equipment filled workshop to a sliding door on the far wall. It opened revealing a small apartment a little larger than her room. "Welcome to my home." He gestured to a transparent chair tucked under a table made of the same material.

Eight Two took a seat and surveyed her surroundings. It was essentially an oversized version of her accommodation. In addition to the bed and desk there was a tiny kitchenette and the extra table and chair. Henry kept his home in the same immaculate condition as his workshop. Not a single item was out of place. The bed was made to a military standard and she could see no personal effects.

"Would you like something to drink?" he asked.

"That would be lovely."

Henry wheeled into the kitchenette and opened a cupboard. "I've got something I've been saving for a special occasion." He rummaged inside. "So, to what do I owe the pleasure?"

Eight Two lowered her eyes to the opaque surface of the table and exhaled slowly. "I needed to talk to someone."

A spoon rattled in a cup. "Been a while since I spoke to anyone who wasn't complaining about something being broken." He turned around with two steaming mugs, rolled across to the table and placed one in front of her.

"What's this?" She took up the mug and sniffed it. The aroma was not something she recognized. She took a tentative sip. It was nutty and sweet, like nothing she had ever tasted.

Henry grinned. "It's called hot chocolate."

"It's delicious."

"Yes, it is."

For a moment she forgot the two children who had died in the village, and was lost in the flavors of the drink. The pleasure was short-lived. The memories flooded back. She locked eyes with Henry and his forehead creased in a frown.

"You want to talk about what happened?"

She gazed into her mug and swallowed back tears. "Today, two children died because of me."

"OK, how did it happen?"

The concerned expression on Henry's face gave her a semblance of comfort as she outlined the events leading up to the explosion. When she was done she dropped her eyes and stared into the empty mug.

"These people are animals. They are turning children into goddamn killers. At least in my day, they gave you a choice." He looked her square in the eye. "You didn't kill those kids, that other guy did."

"I led him straight to them."

Henry sipped from his mug. "You're not like them. None of them have ever given me the time of day." He lowered his drink, leaned across the table and took her hand. "You're the only person in this damn place who even knows my name."

She managed a thin smile.

"Which reminds me. I ain't calling you some number." He wheeled across to his bed and reached into one of the drawers under it. "I had a family once." A book appeared in his hands and he brought it back to the table. "My daughter was like you. She wanted to help everyone." Turning the pages he found a photo and slid it toward her.

Eight Two examined the glossy image. A handsome dark-skinned man in a smart khaki uniform stood with one arm around a beautiful woman. Between them, clinging to the man's leg was a young girl. She had black curly hair, bright eyes and a mischievous smile. Clutched to her chest was a doll. "What happened to them?"

He stared into the distance with glassy eyes. "They were killed in the war of succession. That was a long time ago."

"You were a soldier?"

"A Marine." He rolled around alongside her. "You see that doll?"

"Yes."

"My daughter loved that thing. Found it some place and never let it go. She called it Wilda, Wilda the Lost Girl."

"Wilda," she murmured under her breath. The name was pretty, but that was not what appealed to her. Like the doll, she was a lost girl. "I like that name."

"It's yours. If you want it."

She nodded. "Have you given any of the others names?"

"Yeah, there's asshole, asshat, assface… I can go on."

Wilda giggled. "No, I get the point."

She noticed the corners of his eyes crinkle as he smiled. "Names are for our friends. For people we care for and that care in return. The others, they're not like you. They don't care about anything other than the mission. Sakkin has brainwashed them."

"They're trying to brainwash me too."

He took the empty mugs from the table and wheeled back to the kitchenette. "Well, it isn't working. Do you want another cup?"

"No, I better get back to my room."

"True, I'll give you a lift."

It took her fifteen minutes to find her way back through the vents to her room. When she arrived she lay on the sleeping pad and stared up at the ceiling. Instead of the horror of the murder of the children, she focused on the sense of identity that Henry had given her. Before she finally succumbed to sleep, she swore on her new name to protect the innocent or give her life trying. Eight Two was dead, replaced by an operative with a very different mission, Wilda, the Lost Girl.

Chapter Five

Unknown Village, Kurdistan

A thousand miles from where Wilda slept a brother and sister huddled together before a smoldering fire. Above them the stars shone brightly in a cloudless night sky. Behdin, a brown-eyed fourteen year old boy with an unruly mop of hair, had one arm wrapped around his sister, Xeyal. Two years younger her eyes were bright green and she had a mane of wavy black hair that hung in ringlets down her back.

The pair watched over a flock of their father's goats on a flinty hillside overlooking their village. An antique shotgun lay on the ground next to Behdin, loaded and cocked. It was birthing season and the pair were guarding the newborn kids against jackals. It was a job they took seriously. If even one of the goats were lost it would mean less food for the village to share over the coming winter.

Behdin leaned forward and retrieved a long stick with

which to poke the fire. As he moved, his sister woke from her slumber.

"Is it a jackal?" she asked in her native Kurdish tongue.

He used the stick to push a log into the fire. "No, there's no jackal. Go back to sleep."

She sighed as she cuddled in next to him and fell back asleep.

Behdin wrapped an arm around her and stared out at the horizon beyond the village. As he gazed at the stars he wondered what was past the hills. He had been born in their small village and never ventured further than the next township. One day, when he was older, he was going to climb over the mountain range and explore what was beyond.

As he watched the sky he noticed stars disappearing and then reappearing. He rubbed his eyes and looked again. Now there was a black hole where stars should have been shining. It took him a few more seconds to realize that there was an object in the sky and it was approaching.

He picked up the shotgun as the object grew in size and a faint whirring noise reached his ears. Whatever it was the thing was moving fast. It dipped below the dark bulk of the mountain range but he could hear it getting closer. The whirring increased until it sounded like an overgrown mosquito, hovering over his head.

"What is it?" whispered his sister.

"I don't know," he replied in a low voice as he kicked dirt on the fire. "But I don't think it's good. We'll move the herd closer to town."

His sister bundled up their blankets as he took the shotgun and clambered down the hill to find Jezebel, the nanny goat in charge of their tribe. She was huddled in with the rest of the goats when he found her. Grasping the thick collar around her neck he ruffled her ears. She awoke with a bleat and clambered to her feet. "Come on girl, we need to go."

His sister joined them and the other goats followed as he led Jezebel along a narrow trail that wound its way through the thorn bushes and rocky outcrops that covered the hillside.

Minutes passed and he paused to listen for the flying object. He could not hear it over the noise of the goat's hooves on the trail.

They pushed a little further to a clearing near their village. In the darkness Behdin spotted the stone hut that shepherds used for shelter during the harsh winter. He released Jezebel and the goat immediately found herself a new sleeping spot. The other animals gathered around her and soon they were asleep.

Behdin sat with his back against the outside of the hut and wrapped one arm around his sister. She cuddled in against him and nodded off. He continued to scan the darkness for any sign of the strange object.

Minutes passed and his eyelids grew heavy. His head slumped forward and he jerked it upright, fighting the urge to sleep. It was a short-lived battle and within moments he was gently snoring.

A scant half-hour later Behdin was woken by a faint whistle. The noise reminded him of the kettle on his mother's stove. He reached for the shotgun and climbed to his feet, disturbing Xeyal from her slumber.

"Behdin, what is that noise?"

The whistle had grown to a roar and beyond the village he spotted two pinpricks of blue light against the mountains. They grew in size as the intensity of sound increased and soon a dark shape appeared in the sky.

"Xeyal, hide in the hut. Do not come out until I return," snapped Behdin as he ran toward the village.

He blundered over rocks and through bushes, ignoring the thorns that tugged at his clothes and skin. The black shape stopped and hovered over the fields west of the village near the riverbank.

When he was close he paused, chest heaving, and fired both barrels of the shotgun into the air. The boom echoed off the hills as he cracked the ancient weapon open and stuffed two more cartridges into the breech.

Lights appeared from the town as he turned his attention back to the aircraft. It still hovered over the field, beyond thick bushes. It reminded him of a mountain hawk, waiting for a rabbit to dash from cover. As he aimed the shotgun at it dark shapes dropped from its underside.

His heart pounded as he pushed through the bushes with the gun held ready. As he reached the edge of the field the earth trembled under his feet. He spotted hulking shapes running toward the village, almost invisible, blending into the darkness. Monsters were attacking his people and it was his duty to protect them. Aiming at one of the figures he remembered what his father had taught him and led his target by a hand.

He closed one eye as the shotgun boomed and the flash obscured his vision. Opening his good eye he surveyed the damage.

Fear gripped him as he saw the monster had changed direction. Now it strode directly toward him with one arm extended. The thing had to be a mountain troll or a demon. Its matte-black body seemed to absorb the light around it. His father was a big man, but this thing stood at least two feet taller.

It was less than a dozen yards away when he found the

courage to fire his last shell. The shotgun blasted the monster square in the chest but the beast kept coming.

Behdin opened his mouth to scream as a pulse of blue light emanated from the monster's hand and washed over him. His legs failed and he crumpled to the ground with his mouth open. His stomach heaved and he vomited before slumping sideways and passing out.

The Institute, Jordan

Wilda slid into her allocated immersion pod and waited for the lid to close. She yawned as she made herself comfortable. Despite a lack of sleep she felt energized and ready to take on the day's challenges. In her mind, no longer was she being molded into a mindless killing machine like the others. No, from her perspective she was being equipped for an entirely different mission.

"Welcome, trainee Eight Two, to your virtual training immersion session," announced the familiar voice of the operating system.

She exhaled slowly and was transported to a virtual briefing room. A quick glance around the confined space confirmed that all four of her teammate's avatars were present. She locked gazes with Tree. He glared at her. She smiled pleasantly and winked. The resulting effect was a look of confusion on Tree's face.

A side door hissed open and a black-uniformed Sakkin instructor strode in and positioned himself at the front of the chamber. Behind him the gray wall displayed an overhead image of a sprawling township surrounded by lush green vegetation. "Squad *Gurion*, welcome to the briefing room of the aerostat Liberator."

Aerostat, that explained the tiny briefing room, thought Wilda. Sakkin industries used the airships as mobile operations bases.

"Your mission today is an infiltration operation."

The team released a collective groan, all except Wilda.

"You will each be issued an individual mission. Failure to complete it will directly impact your ranking within the squad for the next phase of training," continued the instructor. "Standby for your intelligence briefing."

The room darkened and the presentation played out on the screens. The level of complexity that had been coded into the scenario amazed Wilda. The village housed over three thousand separate entities each with their own personality, back-story and motivations.

The overarching storyline placed a threat element among the civilian populace. The Red Hand was targeting a local mining operation, Sakkin's client. The miners wanted the group eliminated with minimal collateral damage. Wilda and her team were to infiltrate and identify the leadership of the Red Hand.

Briefing complete she and the others moved through the aerostat's narrow corridors to the hangar bay. Located at the rear of the massive craft the hangar was fifty yards long and half as wide. In other simulations Wilda had seen the bay filled with rows of clankers or even vertjets. This time the hangar and its hinged floor were empty.

She glanced at the rest of her team and noted their avatars were now dressed in baggy black flight suits and parachutes. A quick check of her body reassured her that she was dressed in the same manner. Reaching up she touched her helmet with gloved hands.

Suddenly a flashing red light activated and the floor shuddered as the double doors swung outward and wind whipped into the hold. Wilda and her teammates stood at the edge of the gap gazing down on virtual clouds.

The doors locked open and the light flashed green. She stepped out into the void and enjoyed the sense of weightlessness as she dropped away from the aerostat. Rolling onto her back she looked up at the massive airship as it disappeared into the clouds.

Freefall was one of her favorite parts of training, even in the simulator. High above the world she felt like an eagle soaring far from her worries and the prying eyes of Sakkin. Reality could not be any further from the truth, but she pushed that from her mind as she plummeted toward green fields.

Hours of wind tunnel training meant she carved through the air like a pro. The Heads Up Display in the helmet gave her altitude, speed and marked her designated landing zone.

At five thousand feet she activated her parachute, bracing for the jolt. It never eventuated.

The failed deployment reminded her that the trainers were watching her every move, changing the scenario to challenge her and measure her response. She followed the protocol activating the cutaway via voice control.

An alarm sounded and red lettering flashed in her HUD:

CUTAWAY FAILURE.

Her heart rate increased as she gave the order again. The red words continued to flash in front of her eyes as the altimeter dropped at an alarming rate.

Wilda's heart felt like it was pounding in her ears as she forced herself to concentrate.

The ground raced toward her as she reached behind her head, searching for the flap that held her main chute in place. Her shoulder felt like it would pop as she stretched to reach it.

A second alarm sounded as she raced past two thousand feet. Her gloved fingers finally clutched the nylon cover and she grabbed it, throwing it clear.

There was a roar and a snap as the ultralight wing filled, yanking her out of freefall. Then it snapped free and she dropped. A green field rushed toward her before the reserve caught her fall and she landed with a wet slap in a rice paddy.

She sat gathering herself for a moment before shrugging out of her soaked flight suit and balling it up with her parachute and helmet. Then she struggled out of the muddy field and up a bank of soft black earth. Standing on a raised pathway she wiped her hands on her pants and cleaned her face with her sleeve.

The simulator had dressed her in jeans, boots, a T-shirt and a threadbare camouflage jacket with a strange symbol on the shoulder. As far as outfits went it was practical and comfortable.

Orienting herself to the ground she worked out the direction of the village and walked quickly along a track toward thick jungle.

The level of detail in the simulator always amazed her. It looked, smelled and felt exactly as she imagined a tropical forest would feel. Hopefully one day she would get to experience one for real.

As the jungle thinned iron-roofed shanties appeared among the lush green vegetation. Grubby bright-eyed children played around the chickens and pigs foraging for food. A toddler grinned at her and she returned the smile as she climbed a low rise. As she rounded a cluster of shacks the rest of the village came into view.

She guessed it was modeled on what had once been a bustling city. Disease and violence would have decimated the population and the jungle reclaimed what was no longer needed. What remained was a square mile of vine-covered buildings that reached tens of stories into the sky.

A tall wall surrounded the central hub. Wilda knew, from her briefing, that this was used as a fortress to protect the villagers from marauding warlords. Intel also indicated that the Red Hand had taken control of the citadel in addition to infiltrating the local militia.

As she descended into the outskirts of the township the path widened and foot traffic increased. From the carts and baskets piled high with produce she deduced it was market day. She moved with the flow until she noticed an elderly woman by the side of the trail looking forlornly at a handcart laden with fruit.

As she got closer she could see it was missing a wheel. "Hello, do you need some help?" she asked as she stopped.

The woman's wrinkled features broke into a broad smile and she nodded. "Thank you, thank you."

Wilda inspected the cart and found that the pin holding the wheel in place had sheared. Lifting the cart she slipped the wheel back on and searched for something to replace the pin. As she inspected the cart she spotted a familiar face in the crowd. One of her squad mates had joined the throng of travelers but had not seen her crouched beside the cart.

A piece of wire substituted the pin and soon she and the old lady were pushing the cartload of fruit toward the city gates. As they got closer Wilda saw armed men inspecting the crowd moving through the narrow opening.

Suddenly, shouting filled the air and a figured dashed from the line in front of them. Wilda caught a glimpse of her teammate fleeing down an alley with men in pursuit. Then the figure disintegrated into a million pieces. The gunmen stood confused for a few seconds before returning to their post at the gate. The Sakkin trainee had been compromised and ejected from the simulator.

Her pulse quickened when they reached the gate and the armed men scrutinized them. She felt their eyes linger on her as she helped the old lady push the cart. It jolted to a halt as a heavily muscled thug stepped in front of them and thrust his finger at Wilda.

"Who is this?" he barked.

"She's helping me you big lug. Now, get out of the way, or I'll tell your mother you're being bothersome," the old lady snapped.

The man's eyes narrowed and he begrudgingly let them pass.

Wilda could have hugged the old lady as she guided them along narrow streets shouldered by tall concrete buildings. After a block or so they moved out of the urban canyon into an open square bustling with activity.

She stood for a moment taking in the commotion of the marketplace. Voices filled the air as hawkers hocked their wares. Aromas of roasting meat, spices, herbs, vegetables, flowers and perfumes assaulted her nose as people bustled past.

It all seemed so real, making it easy to forget it was a simulation. A tiny chip at the base of her skull was interfacing with her brain and replicating every sensory aspect of the environment.

"Thank you so much for your help," said the old lady, thrusting a basket of fruit into her arms.

"Oh, I couldn't."

"I insist. No one else stopped to help an old lady in need."

Wilda accepted the gift and hugged her before taking the basket of fruit and setting off on her task to infiltrate the Red Hand. Weaving her way through the market she spied two children sitting in the gutter. They stared forlornly at a stall selling baked goods. Only a few years younger than Wilda the two boys looked similar enough that she assumed they were brothers.

"Hello, do you mind if I sit?" she asked.

One of the boys shrugged. She sat next to them and placed the basket of fruit at her feet. Picking out a juicy mango she peeled back the skin and bit into the flesh. The two boys stared at her as she chewed.

"Would you like one?" she asked, pushing the basket toward them.

The boys nodded as they grabbed the fruit and attacked it with vigor. The three of them slurped at the ripe mangoes as Wilda scanned the crowd for militants.

"Are you going to eat all of those?" asked one of the boys as he finished.

She shook her head. "No, you can have another one."

"Do you mind if we take some to our mother?" the other asked.

"Sure, but I'm going to need some information in return."

The older of the boys frowned. "What kind of information?"

"Nothing too serious. I just want to know where the men who guard the gate like to hang out?"

The boys glanced at each other.

"Why do you want to know about the Red Hand?" he asked.

She shrugged. "I was thinking about joining."

He laughed. "They don't let girls join."

"Why is that?"

"Because girls aren't good fighters," added the younger one.

"Really? And who told you that?"

"Everyone knows it," added the elder.

She let out a sigh and shook her head. Even here in an entirely simulated world she was not free from the prejudices that plagued her in the *Institute*. "You can have the rest," she said rising to her feet.

"It's your fruit. You should come with us," said the younger of the two.

"No, that's OK."

"Are you sure? Our big brother is in the Red Hand. You could ask him if you can join."

Wilda turned and smiled at them. "Really, that would be great."

The older one shrugged. "He's going to tell you the same." He rose to his feet. "But, he'll definitely tell you where they hang out. He loves mangoes."

The two boys led her along a street buttressed with high buildings. For Wilda it was a small victory. She had only been in the simulation for a matter of hours and already she had a lead into the Red Hand. With any luck she would complete the mission early and be able to sneak away and visit her new friend Henry.

Leon Wilken strode into the *Institute's* crescent-shaped operations room and took a seat in his command chair. In front of him, on a lower level, six of his staff sat monitoring a wall of digital screens.

"Status report on the infiltration simulation," he snapped as he studied the monitors.

"Only one trainee remains live. The rest of squad *Gurion* have been compromised and digitally terminated," replied a female staff member.

"Let me guess, trainee Eight Two?"

"Yes sir, she has successfully infiltrated the city and established contact with a low-level enemy operative."

"Of course she has," he mumbled. Marnisha Copeland had added the infiltration sequence specifically to show up his trainees. They were not equipped for intelligence collection. That was the role of other more readily expendable assets. His operatives were trained to coordinate and eliminate, not sneak around making friends with indigenous scum.

"Sir, do you want me to terminate the scenario?"

He considered the option and discarded it. If Copeland found out she would make his life hell. "No, let it run for the time being. Where are we with the preparations for the *Tsalmaveth*?"

"The Homs facility is green for mechops but is running low on Organic Freeplay Targets," announced a male staff member.

"When is our resupply due?"

"The Hunter Team is inbound. Once they arrive we'll have a better understanding of our shortfall. I'm confident that with some creative cross-leveling we will be able to meet all training requirements."

Leon drummed his thick fingers against the armrest of

his chair. "Let's hold off on using OFTs initially. Use the humanoid mechops to fill the gap until we've replenished our stocks."

"Yes, sir."

He rose from his chair. "Right, I'll be in my cabin. Update my flexipad as the simulation unfolds."

The female staff member spoke. "Sir, don't forget the ceremony in the hangar this afternoon."

He paused halfway to the door. Damn, he had completely forgotten the trainee's transition ceremony. He had planned to spend the afternoon entertaining Shona in his room. "Yes of course." The doors opened. "Oh, and ensure the laundry has prepared my uniform."

Chapter Six

Homs, Syria

Behdin's eyes snapped open as an alarm sounded. The high-pitched wailing penetrated his skull, adding to his confusion as he pushed off the smooth hard floor and sat upright. He turned his head, surveying his surroundings through blurred vision.

The last thing he remembered was the black figure bearing down on him. He climbed to his feet and braced against the wall. Nausea swept over him as his legs wobbled and he vomited, the rancid liquid splashing his boots.

Without warning the alarm stopped and one wall of the tiny dark cell slid into the ceiling, revealing a well-lit tunnel.

Gathering himself he peered into the narrow opening. It was sleek and white with glowing panels along the ceiling.

"If you remain in the cell you will be killed," a female voice announced in his native tongue.

"Where am I?" he demanded.

The voice repeated the warning.

Behdin stepped tentatively into the corridor and the door snapped shut behind him. He stumbled as the floor moved and he was transported along the hallway into another cramped cell. This one had strange mechanical arms hanging from the roof.

"Raise your arms above your head," ordered the voice.

He followed the directions and one of the arms raced around him, shining a red light over his body. Above him a circular portal snapped open and two robotic arms holding black objects lowered. One moved to his front, the other his back. Then in one swift movement they locked two halves of a vest together, encasing his torso.

Yelling he clawed at the smooth black material.

"Attempting to remove your armor will result in instant death. It contains an explosive charge that sits over your heart. Failure to follow orders will result in a shock."

The vest emitted a soft whine and then he felt pain like he had never felt before. His muscles convulsed and he cried out, dropping to his knees. It lasted a split second and then it ceased.

"Continued failure to comply will result in death. The vest has an in-built communications system that will issue your directives. If you follow orders and survive, you will be freed. Please exit the chamber and await direction."

There was a hiss and another door opened. He stumbled through it, trembling, and emerged into a dark cavernous space. The filthy floor and rough concrete walls were a stark contrast to the chamber he had left. The earthy smell of mold hung in the air.

A cluster of people sat in the shadows at the far end of the prison. He walked tentatively toward them.

"Behdin!"

He recognized his sister's voice and turned to see her

running toward him. His heart sank as he spotted the black vest that encased her body. Wrapping his arms around her, he fought back tears. "Xeyal, how did they find you? I told you to stay in the hut."

"I heard you yell. I thought you were hurt."

He hugged her even harder.

"What is this place?" she asked.

"I don't know, but if we stay together we will be safe, OK." He released her and used his sleeve to wipe the tears from her eyes. "I promise I'll get us home."

The Institute, Jordan

Wilda took a sip from a mug of hot tea as she sat with the boys, their older brother, father and mother on the rooftop of the concrete block of flats where the family lived. They had invited her in with open arms, enabled in part by the fruit basket, but also by the fact she was a girl. The boy's mother, surrounded by men, had always dreamed of a daughter.

"So, Wilda, where are you originally from?" asked the mother as they watched the sun set over the jungle.

When they had asked for her name, she had used the one Henry had given her. It felt good to hear it from another person's mouth, even if that person was merely a simulation controlled by a supercomputer.

"My parents had a farm out near Maijia. They died when the robots came." She glanced at the eldest brother, the one who was a member of the Red Hand. He shook his head slowly as he drank his tea.

There was an awkward pause before the father spoke.

"Wilda, thank you for bringing the fruit. It was very generous of you to share."

She smiled. "It is my pleasure. Thank you for welcoming me into your home."

The mother got to her feet and started collecting dishes. "If you need somewhere to stay you're welcome to sleep here on the roof."

"That sounds lovely." Wilda helped her carry the plates and cups downstairs to the kitchen. As she turned to return to the roof the older brother grasped her arm.

"Mother, I'm going out. I'm taking Wilda with me," he said, bundling her out of the apartment into the stairwell.

"Where are we going?" she asked as they descended to the lobby.

"You said you're from Maijia?" The boy descended the stairs with Wilda in tow.

"Yes, where the robots are cutting into the earth." Damn, she had not meant that to sound so clichéd.

"Most of the people who know that area are dead. How long ago were you there?"

Wilda recalled the detail of the mine from her intelligence briefing. She was confident she could answer any question regarding the layout and security procedures. "A little over a week."

As they reached the landing he turned to her with eyes shining with excitement. "I'm going to take you to see some people. They're going to ask you many questions. If you tell them the truth you will help avenge the lives of your parents and friends."

"The Red Hand?" she whispered.

He nodded before turning and leading her out of the building. As they entered the street Wilda noticed a flickering light cast across the cracked concrete. It gained in intensity as they walked along. She glanced up, expecting to see a faulty streetlight. There was not. As she looked back at her guide she saw he had turned to face her.

"They're lying to you," he mouthed as he disintegrated into a shimmer of pixels.

One moment she was in the scenario and the next she lay in her immersion pod, back in the *Institute*.

"Computer, please run a system check," she said as she hit the eject button on the side of the pod.

"System is fully functional," said a female voice.

"Then why was I ejected from the scenario? I wasn't compromised."

"Training session has been terminated. Trainee Eight Two you will report to the hangar deck with the rest of your squad."

As she climbed out she saw that the rest of the squad were leaning against the wall or sitting on the floor.

"Finally!" said Tree.

"Sorry to keep you waiting," she said pleasantly. "We've been ordered to report to the hangar."

"We know."

As a squad they made their way out of the immersion classrooms and into the high-speed elevator.

"Did anyone make it into the citadel?" asked Tree.

No one responded.

"What about you, Eight Two? Did you get inside or did you hide in the bushes till the mission ended?"

The doors to the elevator opened.

"I made contact with the Red Hand."

The other members of the squad stared as she strode out of the elevator and into the armory. She glanced into the workshop and shot a smile at Henry who waved back. Passing the clanker and berserker bays she stepped out into the hangar where the other trainees were arrayed in their squads. A staff member directed her and the rest of squad *Gurion* to fall into their position.

Wilda recognized the Head Instructor as he stepped onto a raised platform and stood behind a lectern. He was dressed in a black combat uniform with razor-sharp creases and a bright red beret. Pinned to his barrel chest was an orange ribbon with a silver star beneath it. Every trainee knew the instructor's reputation. He was a highly decorated Israeli special forces operative with authority to terminate their status and their lives. Despite his short stature he was the most feared man in the *Institute*.

"Trainees, today marks a significant milestone in your lives." His voice echoed off the concrete walls of the hangar. "Today you graduate from your current class to the next level. For the seniors this means moving into command positions, and for the rest, it means following them into the *Tsalmaveth*."

As he scanned the ranks of trainees, he paused on Wilda. She met his steely gaze with a defiant look of her own.

"Some of you will not survive this phase. You will not graduate to serve in Sakkin's ranks as the guardians of the ADBLOK."

Wilda felt his eyes boring into hers.

"Those of you that do will finally have the opportunity to repay the debt you owe this great corporation."

Finally, his eyes returned to the lectern.

"He hates you," whispered Tree.

The comment unsettled her. If her teammate had noticed the malice in the Head Instructor's gaze then she had not imagined it. She stood as he allocated each of the senior trainees to their squads and nominated their second-in-command. When he reached squad *Gurion* he assigned Seven Nine Nine as their squad leader. She waited for him to read out Tree's designator. Instead, he read out hers. She was now the second-in-command.

"They're setting you up for a big fall," hissed Tree as the Head Instructor finished his address by giving them the afternoon off.

No one congratulated Wilda as she left the hangar, not even Seven Nine Nine. Her teammates huddled together around Tree. No doubt they were planning how to ruin her opportunity and bring her down. She did not care. It explained why the Head Instructor had stared at her so intently. Clearly he was conducting some kind of experiment on her.

Instead of returning to her room or the recreation level she made her way to her equipment locker. Sitting on a crate she made adjustments to her helmet. She was still there twenty minutes later when everyone else had left.

"Hey, Wilda."

Looking up from her equipment she spied Henry wheeling toward her with a broad smile. "Hello, friend. How have you been?"

"Good, I was wondering if you wanted to help me service a berserker suit?"

She rolled her eyes. "That sounds like hard work."

"Come on. You might learn something."

It took her a moment to stow her equipment before she followed him around to the bays that housed the bulky exoskeletons. She whistled as she saw scorch marks on the chest armor of a suit that hung from its mounting like a battered dinner jacket. "Someone's been in the wars."

Henry activated his flexipad and checked the suit's vitals. "The live fire stuff keeps me on my toes."

She watched as he activated a remote tool arm. It hung from the roof on a rail that allowed it to slide from bay to bay doing all the heavy lifting for the crippled technician. "Henry, why hasn't Sakkin fixed your injury?"

He used the flexipad to manipulate the arm, removing the damaged chest plates. "They can't repair the spinal cord."

"They could interface your brain and give you an exoskeleton for your legs. Then you could move around without your wheelchair."

"Why would they spend millions on me when I can still do the job without it?"

"What about your quality of life?"

"What about it? You really think that Sakkin gives a damn about quality of life? They're all about the bottom dollar. The minute you're no longer profitable they'll toss you like a blown ultracapacitor. Which, I'm thinking, is what is wrong with this bad boy. Come have a look. I'll show you how to remove it without frying the circuits."

Wilda stepped around one side of the suit as Henry wheeled in from the other. She watched as he removed an armored panel and disconnected two hoses. Coolant gas hissed from the couplings as he used a specialized wrench to remove a silver flashlight-sized canister from its recess.

"That wasn't hard."

He shrugged. "Harder in the field without the tools. But, if you ever need a power pack it can be done."

"What about the weapons? Can you strip them off and use them without the suit?"

"Sure can. The railer has its own internal capacitor so it can keep shooting in the event of a suit failure. But it's a lot heavier than your jumper railer, weighs close to thirty pounds. Right, let's run a full diagnostic and see what else is cactus."

It took the pair another half hour to bring the berserker suit back online. When it was done she helped Henry pack away his tools and joined him in his room.

"Henry, why do you work for Sakkin?" she asked as he made hot chocolate. "I'm an orphan. I owe Sakkin my life, but why are you here?"

He passed her a mug. "You don't owe Sakkin shit."

"How can you say that? I remember the raid that killed my mother. I remember a Sakkin operative neutralizing the men who had captured me."

"You remember what they want you to remember."

She frowned.

"Wilda, they control every aspect of your life. What you eat, what you wear, what you do and to an extent, what you feel. Do not, for one second, think they can't reach into your head. They do it with the simulations. Who's to say they can't do it with your memories."

"No, they wouldn't do that. We're all orphans of war, Henry. Why would they take that away from us?"

"Maybe they took you from your families and want you to believe you're orphans." He stared at her with sad eyes. "These people are ruthless, Wilda."

Later that night she lay staring at the sterile white ceiling of her room with Henry's words running loops in her mind. What if he was right? What if Sakkin had taken her from her family and modified her memories to believe her mother was dead? It might be possible that both her father and mother were still alive. The realization steeled her determination. She would graduate from the *Institute* and find the truth.

An icy cold wind swept across the mountains and penetrated her cloak, chilling her to the bone. She stood on a rocky outcrop staring across a barren valley illuminated by the light of a half moon. On the slope opposite a facility nestled into the sheer rock. It could have been an ancient fortress except the walls were vibrant white and the roof capped with massive steel domes that bristled with antennas.

"What is this place?" she whispered.

"This is where it all began," a male voice replied.

The response startled her and she turned to the figure that had appeared next to her. It took her a moment to recognize him as the oldest boy from the simulation. The one who had delivered a message as the program was terminated.

She turned back to the sleek white fortress. "This is where I'm from?"

When there was no reply she glanced back and saw that he was gone. Spinning she searched her surroundings, but there was no trace of him.

A bright flash blinded her and suddenly she was inside a long white hallway. Shouting voices filled the hall as medical staff rushed toward her with a body on a stretcher. She flattened herself to one side as they raced past. Locking eyes with the patient she realized it was someone she knew, her mother.

Wilda followed as they pushed the stretcher along the corridor and through a door. It swung shut as she reached it. Grabbing the handle she tried desperately to gain access, but it was locked. She peered through the door pane. Her mother was being wheeled into a room filled with medical equipment.

"Let me in!" she screamed, bashing on the door. "Let me in!"

A hand grasped her shoulder, startling her, and she turned to find herself face to face with the boy from the simulator. "They're lying to you," he mouthed as he disintegrated into a shower of pixels.

Wilda's eyes flashed open and she found herself back in her room staring at the ceiling. She took a moment to gather her thoughts. If Sakkin were responsible for the dream then for what ends? The company wanted her and the other operatives to believe they were orphans. Why would they fill her head with memories of her mother?

She left her bed and retrieved the notebook from its hiding place in the ceiling. The medical facility in the mountains was significant and she needed to capture it before it faded from her memory.

As she sketched the fortress the face of the boy from the simulator appeared in her mind. Twice now he had warned her that 'they' were lying to her. The strange thing was that it had occurred in a world where Sakkin literally controlled everything. This made her think that they were messing with her mind. What she could not work out was the endgame.

She finished sketching the fortress, slid the book back into the ceiling and returned to her bed. She needed to get some sleep. Tomorrow was the first day of the *Tsalmaveth*, a grueling week of intensive live fire operations. For the first time the targets would be real, and mistakes fatal. Three trainees from the last class had been killed. If she was going to make it through the week and find answers to her questions, she needed to be at the top of her game.

Chapter Seven

The Institute, Jordan

Wilda stood ramrod straight in front of her equipment locker with her fists balled on her thighs and eyes staring ahead. Their new team leader had called the snap inspection during breakfast and squad *Gurion* had abandoned their meals and rushed to the armory.

"A Sakkin operative must always be prepared," bellowed Seven Nine Nine from the far end of the lockers. "While you are under my command your equipment will always be ready. Is that clear?"

"Yes, senior!" Wilda yelled with the other team members.

From the corner of her eye she could see him progressing along the lockers. He paused in front of Tree's, immediately to her left, and briefly inspected his helmet. Then he gave the tall teenager a nod and moved on.

She swallowed as he stopped directly in front of her and

looked her in the eye. "Trainee Eight Two, are you ready for the *Tsalmaveth*?"

"Yes, senior."

He leaned close enough that she could feel his breath on her face. "They made you my second-in-command, but I don't think you've got what it takes to survive, much less lead. I want you to know that if you hold me back, I'm going to do everything in my power to destroy you."

"I won't let you down, senior."

He smirked. "I hope not. For your sake." He stepped away from her. "Squad *Gurion*, our initial briefing will occur in ten minutes. Get your gear organized and don't be late." He turned and strode out of the locker room.

"You are so screwed," said Tree as she grabbed her underarmor and strapped it on. He leaned against her locker. "Everyone hates you Eight Two. Everyone wants you to fuck up during the *Tsalmaveth*."

"Shut up, Tree."

"Even the Head Instructor wants you to die."

His last comment was the final straw. She took a step toward him and grabbed the front of his shirt. Her combat dagger snapped from its sheath. Spinning it over her palm she thrust it at his groin. It stopped with the point touching cloth. "Say another word and I'm going to trim your manhood."

He swallowed.

"You know what they'll call you then?" she whispered.

The taller teenager shook his head.

"Twig. They'll call you twig."

40 Miles West Of Amman, Jordan

As the vertjet swooped in on a derelict city Wilda ran a diagnostic check on her jumper suit. Seven Nine Nine had decided to go with the lighter weight suits. It was a decision she respected, they were easier to maneuver in the tight confines of a city and for this mission they didn't have clankers to slow them down.

Rather than the heavy armor and hydraulics of the berserker they relied on artificial carbon nanotube muscles for strength and protection. The synthetic weave was less than a half-inch thick but made her faster, stronger and harder to kill.

Their mission was seek and destroy. Hunter drones were already active in the city identifying targets. Once the squad landed Seven Nine Nine would allocate them to each team.

Wilda was not particularly happy with who she had been partnered with. She did not trust any of her squad members, but at least they were not openly hostile toward her. Tree, she suspected of plotting her downfall.

"One minute," announced their squad leader. "Don't fuck this up people. The current standing record is sixty-eight minutes. I want all hostiles eradicated inside the hour."

She turned and looked at Tree. His eyes narrowed behind his faceplate then disappeared as he activated the tint. Real mature, she thought as she checked the charge on her hand-held railer.

Unlike the berserkers the lighter weight suit did not have built-in weapons. It also had less ballistic protection. However, it did enable the operator to leap higher and move faster. Wilda valued these attributes more than firepower.

"Thirty seconds," bellowed Seven Nine Nine.

She climbed to her feet and turned to face the ramp, reaching up and grasping one of the grips attached to the roof. The airframe shuddered as it decelerated, sending her internal organs toward the floor. The rear ramp snapped open with a hiss as they hovered above a building.

Blinding bright sunlight lanced into the hold, triggering the tinting in her visor. She followed Tree off the ramp and moved to her designated sector with her weapon held ready.

The vertjet roared into the air, whipping dust from the rooftop. As it streaked away Seven Nine Nine issued his orders. "Hunter drones have identified hostile groups to the north and east. Tree, you will take Eight Two and Three Four and neutralize the northern group. The rest of us will destroy the hostiles to the east."

Wilda was about to point out that she was the designated second-in-command but held her tongue. Seven Nine Nine was the team leader and his word was final.

"A-firm," replied Tree. "Eight Two, let's move out. You're on point."

Gripping her weapon she made for the edge of the rooftop. A quick glance confirmed they were ten or more stories up. Below were the abandoned streets of what had once been a bustling city; another of the Arab capitals annihilated by Israel, in retaliation for the nuclear attack on Jerusalem.

"Take the stairs," ordered Tree.

She shrugged and moved to the stairwell opening. Using the suit's power she tore the door from its frame before tossing a ball scanner into the dark fire stairs.

It took the scanner seconds to confirm that the first two flights of stairs were clear. As she descended her helmet automatically amplified the limited light. It also displayed the video feed from the drone as it bounced toward street level.

"Eight Two, hurry up. I don't want Seven Nine Nine beating us."

She increased her descent down the dusty stairs. It took her less than a minute to reach the ground floor where she recovered her scanner. Pocketing it she forced open the door and moved into what was once the lobby of an apartment building.

She felt a pang of sadness as she spotted dried corpses on the sand-covered floor, caught in an eternal embrace. They would have fallen there when the neutron missile had exploded above the city bombarding them with radiation.

Moving past the bodies she paused in the doorway and waited for the rest of her team. Consulting the mapping system in her HUD she identified a route to the building where the hunter drones had located the hostiles.

There was a clunk behind her and she turned to confirm it was Tree and Three Four. "I've plotted a route to the building next to the target. Might be worth considering a top down assault to take them by surprise."

"Not a bad idea," agreed Three Four.

Wilda was glad he was there. Of the other three members of squad *Gurion*, he was by far the more logical and reasonable.

"It's workable," agreed Tree. "What are we waiting for?"

Wilda led them along a deserted street, past more bodies and the remnants of a city. Cars sat on rotting tires, trash filled the gutters and sand covered the cracked pavement. They moved along the sidewalk, weapons held ready in case the hunters had missed any hostiles.

Behind her faceplate tears glistened in Wilda's eyes as

she spotted three mummified corpses in the back of a sun-bleached sedan, children. They would not have understood the attack. A bright light in the sky would have caught their attention and then their lives would have been extinguished.

"Those are some dried out trads," said Tree, referring to the bodies as traditional humans who had not been augmented by genetic engineering or bionics.

Wilda turned away and gestured to a building on the opposite side of the street. "That's our elevated position. The target building is directly behind it."

"Right, let's get up there then."

It took less than three minutes to climb the twelve stories to the top level of the glass-walled structure and move onto the roof. Wilda edged to the far side and aimed her railer at the structure opposite. According to the hunters there were twelve or more hostiles located inside the eight-story office block.

"How far is that?" asked Tree as he squatted beside her.

"Twelve yards across and twenty-five down."

"A long jump."

"I can do it." She turned to him. "What's wrong, you scared?"

"No. But, you're still on point."

She managed a faint smile. "Cover me."

Pacing the roof she calculated it was nearly thirty yards across; more than enough space for a run up to clear the gap. Readying herself on the opposite side she focused on the lip from which she would leap. Her heart rate increased slightly as she prepared herself, railer gripped tightly in her gloved hands.

"Hurry up," said Tree.

Assisted by the suit she exploded across the roof like an Olympic sprinter and leaped into the open space above the street. The building opposite rose up and she landed three yards from the edge with an almighty thud, executing a forward roll.

As she rose a door burst open and a man wielding an AK appeared. Her HUD painted him red. Instinctively she raised her railer and fired a single round.

The tungsten penetrator cut through him and the wall behind, spraying blood and gore across its surface. Wilda's eyes went wide and she felt like she'd been punched in the stomach. She had never killed a live human before.

But, the man was not dead. He sat up with a gaping hole in his chest and rotated his head as if possessed.

Wilda felt sick as she watched him try to stand. Then, she caught a glimpse of metal through his shattered torso. Relief washed over her as she realized it was not a man but a robot covered in synthetic skin. A railer snapped and the robot's head exploded as Tree appeared next to her. "Damn, they look so real."

There was a thud behind them as Three Four landed.

Tree stepped over the destroyed robot. "Let's get this done."

She fell in behind the two boys, letting them take on the robots as they descended through the building. It was not until she reached the lower levels that she had shaken the shock of the humanoid robot and rejoined the fight.

They eliminated ten targets by the time they reached the ground level and regrouped.

"The others haven't even made contact yet," Tree said as he placed his railer on the concierge desk. "We annihilated them."

"Because of Eight Two's plan," said Three Four.

Tree raised his faceplate and turned to his teammate.

"I'm in command, not her." Something clattered behind a door to their right and he snatched up his weapon.

Wilda and Three Four both aimed their railers.

"Eight Two, check it out."

She edged toward the door, pushed it open and tossed in the scanner.

"Don't mess around. Get in there."

Shaking her head she shoved the door open and stormed inside. It led into a stairwell. As she descended there was a noise below. An alarm sounded, indicating the ball had detected a life form. As she emerged into a dark parking lot cluttered with abandoned vehicles she spotted multiple thermal signatures in the far corner.

Weapon ready she moved between a rusted van and a convertible with a rotted top to get a clear shot. As she eyeballed the corner a savage growl echoed off the walls.

A large brown dog stood between her and a pile of debris, its hackles raised. The trash behind it moved and she spotted another dog and a litter of puppies.

"OK buddy, I'm backing off."

As she stepped away the dog turned and returned to its partner. Wilda felt her heart warm as he nuzzled the bitch and the puppies jumped around his feet.

"How the hell did they survive?" asked Tree from behind her.

"Where there is a will there is a way."

A beep sounded inside her helmet followed by a transmission. "Bravo team this is Alpha. Our targets are destroyed. Eliminate those final hostiles and move to the RV point," ordered Seven Nine Nine.

"They're not hostiles, just dogs," replied Wilda.

There was a pause. "Eliminate them."

"No, they're harmless."

"Eliminate them, now!"

She turned to Tree and shook her head.

"Eight Two are you refusing my order?" asked Seven Nine Nine.

Tree took a step toward the dogs and a soft whine filled the air.

"NO!"

Molten flame jetted from the bottom of his railer engulfing the family of dogs. Their yelps echoed through the parking lot as he hosed them with plasma.

Wilda's hands shook as she raised her railer and fired a single high explosive round into the flames. It detonated, silencing the animals. The concussion blew her and Tree onto their backs.

"What the hell was that?" bellowed Tree as he stood over her. "You could have killed us."

Wilda fought the urge to scream at him as she climbed to her feet. "He told me to do it."

He snickered. "Too late, you screwed it, Eight Two. Now you're done. They're going to terminate you like the worthless piece of trash you are."

The Institute, Jordan

Wilda slid her helmet back into her locker along with her underarmor. She began to unstrap the combat knife from her forearm, then reconsidered. After the incident with the dogs and Tree's threats, it might be better to have a weapon at hand.

The other trainees had already packed away their equipment and headed for the dining facility. She had taken her time, returning her suit, letting them get ahead. The last thing she felt like doing was eating with a team of cold-hearted killers.

Securing her gear she made her way through the armory to Henry's workshop. The wheelchair-bound technician had his back to her, examining a mechop laid out on a counter.

"Hello, Henry," she said flatly as she joined him.

He turned to her with a relieved expression on his face. "Wilda, I was worried something had happened to you."

"He killed a family of dogs this time," she said. "Mother, father and all the puppies."

He looked confused. "Who?"

"Tree, he slaughtered them like they were nothing."

Henry reached across and took her hand. "Sakkin has turned them into mindless killers, Wilda. You should be thankful that you're still human enough to feel. To mourn the loss of living creatures."

"I won't let them do that to me." Tears streaked her cheeks. "I won't take innocent lives for them."

Henry grasped her hand tighter. "They're going to order you to do exactly that and you'll have to decide if you're going to defy them and face death, or follow their orders and live with the shame."

He shook his head. "I once made a decision that cost the lives of an entire family. It's not as cut and dry as your situation. But their deaths are something I think about every day."

"If you had your time again would you make a different decision?"

"Of course, but that can't happen."

She wiped the tears from her eyes. "It can for me."

Henry nodded. "You do what you have to do. I'll help

you any way I can. Which reminds me, for the next phase of the *Tsalmaveth* you'll be operating in a place called Homs. I've never been there, but I do know the place is a comms nightmare. The lag back to the command center here can be a few minutes."

"That's good to know." She gestured to the mechop. "What can you teach me about their operating system?"

He smirked. "What do you want to know?"

"Everything."

"Right, well let's start with the basics. All Sakkin equipment runs the same operating system. They call it Corecom, I call it Swiss cheese."

"Why?"

"Because it's full of holes. The security's good from the outside but inside is a different matter." He took his flexipad from the counter and held it aloft. "With this, I can control every bit of kit they have, mechops, railers, drones and even the vertjets. As long as it's in uplink range. It's good to go."

"Can you teach me?"

"Depends on what you know about hacking and coding."

"I broke into the maintenance and life support software."

His eyebrows rose. "You got into life support? How did you manage that?"

She shrugged. "I found an admin pad and used its protocols. The data servers have proven more difficult. But, I'm confident I can eventually gain access."

"OK, getting in is the easy part." He nodded toward the mechop. "We'll try out some basics and see how far you get. You like music?"

She nodded. "Yes, there's a collection in the facility library."

Henry grinned. "That crap's not real music. I'm going to show you how to get classics like Beyoncé and Rihanna rocking in your battle suit. Trust me, it's gonna change your life."

Leon strode through the operations room into the briefing facility where Shona Demski waited. The door closed as he dropped into a chair and tossed a flexipad on the table.

"I told that bitch, Eight Two was a liability."

The blonde psychologist nodded. "She's becoming more and more erratic. This latest act of insubordination is the final straw. My recommendation is for immediate termination."

He drummed his fingers on the table. "That's not going to happen. If we put her down, Marnisha will destroy us."

"Leon, you're the head trainer, your decision will not be questioned."

He laughed. "You're as naïve as you are pretty. Marnisha is Manfred Lisker's right hand."

"Lisker?"

He shook his head in disbelief. "The Chairman of Sakkin Industries, the most powerful man outside of the ADBLOK. Your boss."

"Oh, him. Surely he will listen to you?"

"No, he will have endorsed her project." He paused. "Can we make adjustments to her psychological profile?"

Shona consulted her flexipad. "No, she's locked us out. I can monitor her levels, but I can't make any adjustments."

"Her dreams?"

"I can see they are traumatic, but I can't see the inputs. Copeland has all her messaging preloaded and locked."

"Then we've got nothing we can work with."

She flicked a loose strand of hair from her shoulder. "Not exactly."

His eyes narrowed. "What have you got?"

She poked at her flexipad then gestured to one of the walls. An image from a security camera appeared on the screen. It showed trainee Eight Two talking to the crippled technician who ran the facility's repair workshop. "She's developed a friendship."

Leon rocked back in the chair. "What's the nature of this friendship?"

"They meet regularly and have long discussions. She's struggling with the stress of training and appears to be using him as emotional support."

"Bring up his record."

It took her a moment to find the file and bring it up on the screen. Leon scanned through it. "Henry Buchanan has been with the company for twenty-five years. Five of those have been here at the *Institute*. Before that, he served in the US Marine Corps. He lost the use of his legs in a helicopter crash during the War of Succession. His wife and child were killed during the battle of Jacksonville. Served in Afghanistan and Iraq before that." He looked at Shona. "I wonder what he's been telling her."

"I could question him and find out."

"No, leave him be."

Her ageless features took on a surprised expression. "I don't understand, this is a weakness that we can exploit. This may be a perfect opportunity to get rid of Eight Two and undermine Marnisha."

He rose from the table. "Correct, and when the time comes, I will do exactly that. In the meantime, let her cry to the cripple."

Cape Town, South African Zone

Eight thousand miles away, on the other side of the planet, Marnisha Copeland popped the bubble canopy on an autonomous quadcopter and stepped out of it onto a circular landing pad. As she walked away from the aircab its electric-powered blades spun and it lifted off the thirty-story pad and flew away.

The pad jutted from the side of the Sakkin Industries headquarters in the former South African city of Cape Town. Now walled off from sprawling townships the city had transformed into a high tech oasis on a continent of conflict and suffering.

The wind tugged at her skirt and jacket as she paused on the walkway that linked the landing pad to the towering structure. In the distance, beyond a hundred foot high wall, in the half-mile death zone that surrounded the city, a thin column of smoke smudged the horizon. She grimaced, probably another group of trads trying to cross from the morass into the ADBLOK. The drones and mechops would have made short work of them. She pushed the thought from her mind as she passed through a set of thick blast doors into the bustling headquarters of the world's largest security firm.

Established in 2015, Sakkin Industries had invested heavily in autonomous and genetic technologies that had allowed it to thrive in a world plagued by terrorism and conflict. Doctor Copeland had headed the genetic research division since its inception and was now one of the most influential members on its board. The only person above her in the hierarchy was the chairman.

She rode an elevator to the highest point of Sakkin Tower, the executive level, and made her way to the boardroom. Four men were already seated at the table: Andrew Dunbar, the Head of Intelligence, Dominik Skarvin, the Head of Operations, Avi Lerner, the Head of Covert Operations, and Manfred Lisker, the Chairman.

She had known the former Mossad director for over forty years and in that time he had not aged a day. Genetic modification had returned the thick black hair of his youth. He wore it in a neat part over his intelligent gray eyes and hawkish nose.

The chairman made a point of checking his watch as she took the seat to his right. "Marnisha, nice of you to join us." He waited until she was comfortable then nodded to his Head of Operations. "Dominik, let's get started."

She turned her attention to the handsome man who sat opposite. She had enjoyed a short but sordid affair with him a few years back. His blue eyes shone vibrantly and his teeth were perfectly straight, whiter than porcelain. She also knew that beneath his well-cut suit was a rock-hard body.

"Two days ago," began Skarvin in his thick South African accent, "a RESDEC operation in Guatemala was attacked."

As he spoke, images appeared on the far wall. Marnisha recognized a burning structure as a Resource Delivery Conglomerate, or RESDEC, mining outpost.

"Our security contingent was decimated." Skarvin consulted his flexipad. "We lost eighteen mechops and four ganics. Casualties amongst the RESDEC workers were minimal. However, all key equipment was destroyed."

She watched Lisker as the information was delivered. His eyes narrowed and the corner of his mouth twitched. "Do we know who did it?" he asked.

Dunbar, the Head of Intelligence shook his head. "No, sir. At this stage, we're unable to identify the RHE."

RHE was the designator given to a Rival Hostile Entity. Recently an unknown force had been running rings around their security operations. This was the third facility that had been neutralized in the last six months.

"It's them," stated Avi Lerner. The Israeli was Lisker's right-hand man and the head of the covert operations division. Like the chairman he had previously been a Mossad operative. Unlike Skarvin, his bulging arms were not a result of genetic enhancement. He was a lethal fighting machine honed by decades of combat experience.

"There's no evidence to suggest Lascar's involvement," replied Dunbar. The intelligence officer's lean features remained impassive.

"Bullshit," snapped Avi. "My people found a purifier in a village not a dozen miles from that rig."

"And you kept that from us, why?" asked Skarvin. "I could have reinforced our defenses."

Marnisha smiled. With genetic enhancement men no longer suffered from decreasing testosterone levels. Yes, it made them voracious lovers, but it also meant meetings occasionally degenerated into verbal slinging matches.

Lisker barked next. "It wouldn't have made a difference. They would have struck at another location. They know we don't have enough resources to protect every project." He turned to the Head of Intelligence. "I've spent millions on intel collection and you still haven't pinned this to Lascar."

Dunbar shrugged. "They've got support within the ADBLOK. California alone provides over a billion dollars a year for medical clinics and water purification. They're definitely channeling some of those resources into paramilitary operations."

"No shit," added Avi.

"My intelligence that they're headquartered in Abu Dhabi is solid," continued Dunbar. "Perhaps you can provide us an update on your targeting operation?"

She watched Avi carefully as he ignored the question. She knew that, so far, his operatives had no luck locating Lascar's covert base.

He turned to face her. "Have we resolved the issues with our next generation of ganics?" he asked, referring to their genetically-enhanced trainees.

She smiled pleasantly but inside she seethed. Deflection was one of Avi's favorite tricks. "We've made the necessary adjustments to training. The next graduates will be more suited for clandestine operations."

"That better not compromise their operational capability," snapped Skarvin. "I need replacement ganics to cover our security requirements."

Avi fixed him with an icy stare. "Your ganics lack the adaptability to deal with the current threat. They lack the flexibility to defeat an enemy who is smarter and faster."

Skarvin snickered. "So more like your rag-tag trad mercs? Yes, they have been so successful in defeating Lascar and their puppets. My operations are the bedrock of this company's profits and I need ganics that follow orders."

"Enough!" Lisker interjected. "The Lascar problem must be resolved. I will not tolerate any additional excuses. Dunbar, I want to know which of our projects are in close vicinity to Lascar activities. Skarvin, I want you to increase security at these sites and Avi, I want you to penetrate Abu Dhabi."

"Sir, I–," said Dunbar.

Lisker held up his hand as he looked down at his flexipad. "You may leave gentlemen."

Marnisha remained seated as the three men left. Avi was last out the door and shot her a questioning glance before disappearing.

Never one for small talk Lisker initiated the conversation, "Wilken's latest report on your prodigy is particularly damning." His eyes remained glued to his flexipad.

"Leon is a foot soldier, not a strategist."

"He's our best trainer."

"He trains mindless killers and tactitards. Project Eight Two is a finely tuned program with sophisticated outcomes far beyond his basic comprehension. I intend to minimize his input as our timeline progresses."

He looked up. "You mean if your little pet survives the *Tsalmaveth*. Marnisha, this has been an expensive experiment. I've half a mind to cancel your funding."

She shrugged. "That would be a poor choice. The project is nearing completion."

"When can I expect results?"

Marnisha smiled as she folded her hands in her lap. "Your three little stooges play the short game. We both knew this solution was never going to be fast."

He stared directly into her eyes for a moment. Marnisha had no idea what he was thinking. Lisker was the type of man that was always one step ahead. A brilliant strategist he had commanded Mossad's *Kidon* assassination teams before forming Sakkin.

"Very well, the project will continue." He lowered his eyes to the flexipad. "In the meantime, you'll increase the output of standard operatives. We need more of them to protect us from Tariq Ahmed's protégés."

She frowned. "Who is Tariq Ahmed?"

He glanced up. "The former CEO of Lascar Logistics, the company that ultimately became Lascar."

"You know him?"

"I knew him. A long time ago." He stared through the room's windows, out over the wall and into the desert. "A very long time ago. His firm worked for Mossad. Then he betrayed me and was neutralized."

"But his people fight on?"

Lisker nodded then focused back on his flexipad. "That will be all."

Marnisha rose and departed the conference room. As she crossed the foyer she ordered another aircab with her smartwatch. By the time she reached the landing area the craft would be waiting. She would fly past her apartment and grab a change of clothes before heading to the Sakkin airport. If she moved fast she would be at the training facility before the start of the next phase of *Tsalmaveth*. As an afterthought she ordered the watch to download everything they had on Lascar to her flexipad. Lisker's comments intrigued her and she would have plenty of time to read on the flight.

Homs, Syria

Xeyal sat huddled in a filthy blanket in a dark corner of the concrete space. She stared up at the dim lights that hung from the ceiling as she wondered why she had been brought here.

It seemed like days since she and her brother had been taken from their village. A tear formed in the corner of her eye as she thought of her family. If the robots had not killed them they would be desperately searching for her and Behdin.

A hiss from the wall opposite caught her attention. A door had opened and a moment later another victim stumbled into view. It was an elderly man and, like everyone else, he wore one of the black vests. People had regularly been arriving since she had been processed. There were now over forty prisoners.

She watched as the man tore at the vest in a futile attempt to remove it. She had done the same thing, with no success.

"Xeyal, look what I found." Her brother Behdin appeared holding a plastic bag. He'd gone to scrounge for food. Squatting he took a bottle of water and a metallic sachet from the bag and handed it to her. "There's a slot on the other side where food arrives. There are men making sure everyone gets a share."

She made room for him to sit and tore open the sachet. A delicious meaty scent wafted up her nose as she inspected the contents.

"It's some kind of dried meat," he said as she sniffed it.

Biting the rubbery substance she chewed tentatively. It tasted similar to the dried goat that her mother made.

"I listened to some of the men speaking. They said there's a door at the other end that opens and people have to walk through it."

"Where does it go?"

"To freedom."

She finished the meat and reached for her brother's hand.

He held it firm. "Don't worry, Xeyal. I am going to get us home, I promise. Now, drink the water and eat up. You'll need your energy." He made to rise.

"Don't go."

"We need more food."

"Just stay for a little while, I don't want to be alone."

He reached across and brushed a strand of hair behind her ear. "When you've drunk all the water and eaten the rest of the meat, we'll go together."

She smiled flashing the gap in her teeth. "OK."

As she ate, he sat staring at the door to nowhere.

Chapter Eight

The Institute, Jordan

This time when the first explosion sounded Wilda leaped from her bed and grabbed a railer that leaned against the wall of the hut. She stood confused for a moment before recognizing her childhood home. It was a dream.

The door to her room opened and a woman dressed in threadbare combat vest and cradling an old-fashioned assault rifle stood in the opening. As her eyes adjusted to the gloom Wilda recognized her mother. Her long hair was up, almond eyes flashing with fire, and her jaw set.

"Are you ready?" she asked in Arabic.

Another explosion shook the tin walls of the ramshackle hut. "Ready for what?" she asked.

Her mother frowned. "To protect our people." Then she turned and exited the room.

Wilda followed her outside as a volley of rockets screamed overhead and detonated beyond the village. She had been here before, many times, except things had changed. No longer was she a child paralyzed by fear. Now she could fight back.

Her mother signaled toward the center of town. "This way."

"No, they come from the hills."

A mob of screaming villagers ran past them as an explosion blossomed deep in the town.

"How do you know?"

"I've been here before."

Her mother stared at her then nodded. "Lead the way."

She turned and ran with the growing crowd of villagers streaming toward the river. Glancing up at the sky she spotted the Guardian Star and used it as a reference point.

Rounds sliced through the air as she crested the rise before the river. She spotted half a dozen flashes from the far bank as she dropped to a knee and raised the railer. The weapon's thermal scope made it easy to locate her targets and she fired back.

Hooded figures fell like bowling pins as she ruthlessly cut them down. A sharp crack sounded from next to her and she glanced sideways at her mother, also returning fire.

Working together they quickly annihilated the attacking force before they could inflict any more casualties on the fleeing villagers. As Wilda engaged the final target she heard the familiar roar of a vertjet passing overhead. "Help is here?"

In the moonlight she saw her mother frown. "Help? They've come for our children." Her mother turned and ran back to the burning village.

Wilda gave chase, weaving in and out of the people fleeing the onslaught. Smoke hung thick in the air as she sprinted along a narrow alley fenced by ramshackle tin dwellings.

As she reached the edge of the town square she saw the first of the mechops. The dark robotic figures had made short work of the attackers within the village. She could see a cluster of children being attended by the female medic she remembered from her dreams.

She glanced around, searching for her mother and the man who had previously rescued her. Suddenly, an MX22 swooped in over the town square and hovered. Dust, sand, trash and smoke whipped through the air as it landed. She squinted and heard yelling and screaming.

Through the haze she spotted figures being herded up the ramp of the aircraft. Her mother appeared next to her with her weapon aimed at the jet.

"They're taking the children!" her mother yelled as she fired at one of the mechops.

It took Wilda a moment to realize it was the truth. Sakkin operatives were not rescuing the children. They were kidnapping them. She hefted her railer as one of the lethal robots turned and fired. She felt the projectiles whip past her head.

From the corner of her eye she saw her mother crumple to the ground. Then pain shot through her legs and they collapsed under her. She fell on her side, face to face with her dying mother.

"Don't let them take the children," her mother managed before her eyes glassed over.

As Wilda reached out to her she heard the familiar sound of an exoskeleton approaching. She rolled onto her back, reaching for the railer as a figure stood over her. Looking up past the muzzle of a pistol Wilda recognized the face of the man who had saved her in every other dream. He squeezed the trigger.

Wilda's eyes snapped open as her hands touched her face. They came away wet, not with blood but with tears. She sat for a moment gathering herself before climbing onto her desk and retrieving her notebook. Flicking through the pages she found the picture she had drawn of her mother and sat staring at it.

This dream had seemed far more real than any other. Her mother's death felt like a knife had been plunged into her chest. She wiped away the tears as she remembered her last words, "Don't let them take the children."

Unlike every other dream this one did not fade. She could remember every aspect of it, almost as if it had actually happened. Was this a memory that had broken through the dreams seeded by Sakkin? Was she one of the children shepherded into the back of the vertjet?

She turned to the page where she had drawn the man who at first had saved her. The memory that burned brightest was now staring at the barrel of this man's pistol. He was not the hero she originally thought. He had kidnapped her from her family.

An alarm announced the start of the day and she slid the notebook into the thigh pocket of her uniform. Something told her she wanted it nearby. Today was one of the final stages of the *Tsalmaveth* and there was every chance that Sakkin would ask her to take an innocent life. If that order was given, she may never return to the *Institute*. She managed a grim smile as she dressed. At least now, thanks to Henry, she had a way to fight back.

Homs, Syria

Behdin sat with his back pressed against a cold concrete wall, with Xeyal's head in his lap. He'd lost all track of time since they had arrived. The dim lights above glowed permanently and there were no windows.

He and his sister had explored every inch of the prison. It consisted of a single massive space with smaller rooms joined by narrow tunnels. In one of these rooms they had found a basic bathroom with running water. The others had led to storage areas where other prisoners had set up camp.

Behdin had found men who spoke Arabic, a language his mother had taught him. From them he'd learned that there were people from many lands in the prison. However, no one had been able to tell him why they were here, or what was going to happen to them. Exhausted from their ordeal he and Xeyal had found a spot close to a large group and tried to rest.

Behdin held his sister tight as his thoughts turned to his father and the village. He hoped that his warning had saved them. The fact there was no one he knew in the prison was reassuring but also intimidating. He and Xeyal felt utterly alone.

A loud beeping interrupted his thoughts and he glanced around, searching for the source. Out the corner of his eye he spotted a flashing green light in a huddle of sleeping bodies. A strange metallic voice sounded from the light. "Move to the exit tunnel."

A middle-aged man climbed to his feet as the people around him woke.

"You have thirty seconds to comply," announced the voice.

A woman hugged the man with tears streaming from her eyes. He wrapped his arms around her.

On the far wall the freedom door had opened. A bright orange light above it flashed lazily, casting a rotating orange glow.

"Ten seconds."

The man released his wife and turned toward the door. Behdin frowned; he would have to run if he was going to make it.

The man dashed for the opening.

Behdin counted down in his head: 4, 3, 2, 1.

He was still short of the gap when a loud crack sounded and the man dropped like a shot goat.

The woman screamed and ran to the crumpled body.

Xeyal raised her head from his lap. "What happened?"

"Nothing."

As he shielded her eyes from the corpse his own vest emitted a loud beep and delivered the same ultimatum the dead man had received. Behdin helped his sister to her feet and quickly hugged her. "Xeyal, I have to go through the door. If your vest beeps, you will have to go too. I'll find you on the other side."

Tears welled in his sister's eyes.

"Be strong. I'll find you. I promise."

As the vest gave him the thirty-second warning he pried himself from his sister's embrace.

"Don't go," she cried as he left.

He ran past the body of the fallen man and his wailing partner, and reached the door with seconds to spare. Turning he gave his sister a final wave. "I'll find you," he yelled as he stepped back through the door. When he was inside it snapped shut, plunging him into darkness.

The floor rumbled and moved sideways. Behdin braced himself against the wall as it jolted to a halt. Lights flickered on down a corridor and he walked tentatively into a long room with metal sections on either side.

A panel disappeared into the roof revealing a locker filled with clothes and equipment.

"Take the items from the locker and move to the next room," a tinny voice announced from his vest.

He peered inside and found a battered AK-47, a chest rig full of magazines and a khaki headscarf.

"Take the equipment," insisted the voice.

Behdin tentatively removed the harness and headscarf. Finally, he took the assault rifle and inspected it. He was familiar with the venerable Russian weapon. His father had taught him to shoot a variety of guns from when he was twelve. He never really liked the assault rifles, preferring the accuracy of his father's hunting rifle.

With his new equipment in hand he walked along another corridor. For the first time since they had been taken from their village Behdin felt a glimmer of hope. At the end of the tunnel he saw sunlight. Shielding his eyes he stepped out into the back of a truck. Men he recognized from the prison occupied bench seats on either side. Like him they carried weapons and wore a variety of harnesses laden with ammunition.

The truck was open topped and he glanced around, hoping to spot a landmark. Drab concrete walls reached up to the dusty brown sky.

"There's no way out," said an elderly man with a thick brown beard and intense eyes.

The truck jolted forward with the hum of electric motors. Behdin took a seat beside the man.

They climbed a ramp and turned out into a landscape completely alien to Behdin. Buildings twenty times the size of his father's home reached up into the sky. Entire walls had been blasted away with gaping holes in every surface. Rubble and rusted vehicle shells lined the streets.

"I came here when I was a boy," said the bearded man next to him.

"Where are we?" asked another.

"This is the city of Homs. Or at least what is left of it."

"Homs," mouthed Behdin as the truck came to a smooth halt. The tailgate lowered with a hiss of hydraulics revealing two black figures. He raised the AK as he recognized them as the robots that had kidnapped him and his sister.

"Leave the vehicle, move into the building opposite and await instructions," emitted one of the robots. "Failure to comply will result in termination."

Behdin followed the other men into a rubble-strewn foyer. The robots followed them inside then stood motionless at the exit.

"What do they want us to do?" he whispered to the bearded man.

"That part is obvious my son." The man nodded at the AK Behdin held. "They want us to fight."

The Institute, Jordan

Wilda stood in front of her allocated berserker suit holding her flexipad. Her gloved fingers tapped the screen as she accessed the suit's central code. She smiled as she worked. It had not taken long for Henry to teach her the basics. Now, she had an element of independence in Sakkin's tightly controlled world.

"What are you doing?" Tree's demanding tone startled her.

"I'm running a diagnostic."

"Yeah, well hurry up. Seven Nine Nine wants a word with you before we roll out."

The look on his face told her she was due for another threat from their illustrious leader. She finished with the flexipad and slid it into a pouch on the chest armor of the suit.

"Where is he?"

"Over by bay twelve," he said over his shoulder as he walked away.

She found the team leader already wearing his suit. His eyes bored into her from beneath the raised faceplate

"For some unknown reason you haven't been scrubbed from the program despite your actions. What's more, my request to have you removed from my team has been denied," he said.

Wilda made to speak but he cut her off with a raised mechanical gauntlet.

"I want you to know that if your actions in any way compromise my graduation, I'll kill you. This is my *Tsalmaveth* and I won't have you or anyone else screwing it up."

The determined set of his jaw told Wilda he meant it. She swallowed as nodded.

He stared at her for a moment longer then dismissed her with a wave.

As she returned to her own bay and climbed into her

suit she realized the conundrum of her situation. In the very near future she was destined to choose between taking a life and sacrificing her own.

Striding out of the bay she clunked her way through the armory toward the hangar.

Examining her railer she wondered if she had what it took to kill another human being, to aim the lethal weapon and obliterate them with the touch of a button.

The door to the hangar snapped open and Wilda found herself face to face with a beautiful woman dressed in a business suit. Assuming she was a Sakkin executive Wilda stepped to one side. The woman eyed her as they passed and continued on her way.

As Wilda climbed into the waiting MX22 she glanced around at the other members of her team and realized she felt very little for them. They were brainwashed killers and she would happily sacrifice them to save a single innocent life. She wondered if that realization made her one of them. Had Sakkin succeeded in destroying what little humanity remained in her young mind?

The whine of the vertjet's thrusters filled the cabin and she activated the noise canceling circuit in her helmet. A moment later the soulful beats of one of Henry's favorite artists sounded from the speakers. Behind her faceplate she smiled. Sakkin may have abducted her, tried to crush her spirit and wipe out her humanity, but they had also inadvertently provided her with salvation. Ultimately friendship would be the most powerful weapon in her arsenal.

Leon sat in his command chair watching the progress of squad *Gurion's* MX22 on a digital map. Seated at their screens his operations staff managed the insertion of the last of the OFTs, Organic Freeplay Targets. Behind him the door to the facility hissed open and a shapely female figure entered.

Leon turned and met the Sakkin scientist's steely gaze with a smirk. "Good morning, Doctor Copeland. Come to see how your little pet fares in the *Tsalmaveth?*"

"I'm here to ensure the training remains impartial," she replied curtly as she surveyed the room.

He gestured to an empty terminal. "Feel free to take a look at the training program. All of our organic targets are in location and awaiting the arrival of squad *Gurion*."

Marnisha placed her bag down and sat at the terminal. "I saw the report you submitted to Lisker."

He shrugged. "I was succinct and to the point. The Chairman asked for my assessment."

"The psychological update was a nice touch. It's a pity that your little plaything is about as well versed in cognitive science as you are in strategic analysis."

Leon frowned. "Shona has contributed more to the development of our trainees than any other—"

She cut him off with a withering glare. "You forget yourself, Leon. Manfred Lisker and I conceived this program, created it, nurtured it and made it what it is today. My only regret is placing it in the hands of simpletons who don't have the vision to see what the future holds." She turned to the wall map. "When do they arrive in Homs?"

One of the staff replied, "In two hours, ma'am."

"Excellent, I'll return then." She rose, took her bag and made for the door.

Leon waited for the door to shut then let out a sigh. "That woman is a total ball buster. What's the status of our OFTs?"

"Final orders have been sent," replied one of the staff.

"Any more failures to comply?"

"No sir."

Leon chuckled as he rose. "Never is after the first one." He turned to the door. "Page my room when *Gurion* is a half hour from the target."

Chapter Nine

Homs, Syria

Wilda knelt and covered her sector as the vertjet disappeared into the blue sky. Her HUD said it was a little after midday and already a hundred and fifteen degrees. The temperature would be crippling without the cooling systems built into the berserker suit.

Seven Nine Nine issued his orders and they set off toward the target building. The mission was simple; kill or capture a high profile criminal responsible for targeting a mining operation outside of the city. Intelligence was light, which is why their squad leader had chosen to insert on the outskirts of the city and move in on foot.

Wilda was not surprised when she had been put on point. It was the most exposed position within the squad and hence the most dangerous.

She patrolled at a steady pace along the rubble and sand strewn roads. A hunter drone scanned the streets ahead and another hovered three blocks away over the target building.

Wilda knew from experience that the drones had limited range when it came to detecting hostiles. Anyone inside the tall buildings on either side of the street could remain hidden and ambush them as they approached.

"Eight Two, you're moving too slow. Get a hustle on," transmitted Seven Nine Nine.

Wilda shook her head but complied, accelerating to ten miles an hour.

According to the intelligence briefing the city of Homs was a rabbit warren of hostile activity. Ravaged by decades of conflict the buildings were little more than rubble and empty husks. The streets were littered with the refuse of war: empty shell casings, jagged shrapnel, craters and sun-bleached bones.

She arrived at an intersection and crouched behind the blackened remains of what her suit designated as a Russian built BMP fighting vehicle. As she scanned ahead a flicker of movement caught her attention.

Turning her helmet she scanned the upper level of the five-story building opposite. Her sensors failed to detect anything among the debris, but she could not shake the feeling that they were being watched.

"Eight Two, what's the holdup? Do you have eyes on hostiles?"

She turned her attention back to the street. "Negative, the route looks clear." She stepped off, sticking to the shaded side. Glancing back she saw the friendly force HUD markers that showed her the rest of the squad were following her lead. Without the markers they would have been almost impossible to spot, their adaptive camouflage blending with the shadows and concrete.

A red marker hovered above the target building less

than three hundred yards distant. It was a multi-level structure flanked on both sides by buildings of the same height.

Her suit detected the shot a split second before it impacted her armor. The heavy caliber round failed to penetrate but knocked her backward. "Contact with hostiles," she reported as she ducked into cover.

Behind her a railer spat hypervelocity rounds at the shooter.

"Tree, take it out," snapped Seven Nine Nine.

She turned and saw Tree step out from cover. A plasma launcher slid from his back onto his shoulder and locked in place. A rocket streaked skyward and a split-second later an explosion flashed in the upper levels of a building opposite the target.

Gunfire and explosions lashed the street from a second building. Wilda ducked behind a wall as shrapnel pinged off her armor. She raised her arm and fired a volley of smoke grenades. In a matter of seconds thick gray smoke billowed between the buildings, obscuring them from the shooters above.

"Eight two, you will clear the defensive position and provide a diversion. The rest of the squad will assault the primary objective," transmitted Seven Nine Nine.

She grit her teeth; their glorious leader was not even trying to mask his attempts to get her killed.

"Move now," he ordered.

Wilda's new target appeared in her helmet along with the squad's objective. Rolling her eyes she dashed into the cloud of smoke before it thinned. As she reached the base level of the building she realized she had been given a unique opportunity. The only way anyone could see what she was doing was through her suit's cameras and sensors.

And now, because of Henry, she had total control over the exoskeleton's systems.

Eight stories above the smoke-filled street Behdin stalked through the blackened remains of an office. AK held ready, he moved toward the far corner then paused. A smell like burning flesh wafted into the room. Ahead of him, where previously there had been a sniper pair, was now nothing but smoldering debris.

"They're dead," he mumbled. Icy fingers of fear gripped him as he recognized a charred body among the blackened concrete and molten glass. It was one of the men from the truck.

"Your mission is to defend this building," announced the voice from his vest. "If you are successful you will be set free."

He had heard the message no less than twenty times since they had arrived that morning. He was beginning to think that whoever had put them here was no longer monitoring them.

Footsteps from behind startled him and he whipped around.

"Steady son," said the bearded man. "Someone is attacking us. The safest place is high ground."

Behdin nodded and followed him into the central stairwell. The others must have opted to stay below. Armed with rocket launchers and explosives they had barricaded the lower level.

"Where are you from?" the man asked as they climbed.

"My town is called Kare."

"I've never heard of it. Were you captured alone?"

They stepped through a doorway into the next level.

"No, they brought me here with my sister."

"Ah, yes, the girl who was with you in the prison."

Behdin cringed at the thought of his little sister alone in that place. A tear ran down his cheek. He quickly wiped it away.

"Well, this is as good a place as any," the bearded man said as he sat against a wall.

"I will go to the edge and see what is happening."

"Try not to get yourself shot." The man fished a packet of cigarettes from his pocket.

Leaving him to smoke Behdin made his way to the edge of the building. As he crept forward glass crunched under his boots. He crouched behind the window ledge before peering over.

As he scanned the building opposite he heard a faint buzzing, not unlike a giant wasp. He spotted a black disk hovering between his building and the one opposite. He recognized it as one of the objects that had appeared the night of the kidnapping. It had led the robots to his village.

Balancing his rifle on the wall he aimed at the object. "Aim true, exhale and squeeze," he repeated his father's words.

The rifle barked once and the drone sparked. It teetered in the air before tumbling into the street below.

"What have you done?" yelled the bearded man. "Get away from there, you fool!"

As he turned and ran something shrieked through the air. Hot air blasted his face and chips of concrete stung his arms and legs as he fell forward. He scrambled for cover, glass shards tearing at his hands and elbows.

He felt a hand grab his vest and drag him toward the stairwell.

"Go, go, go!" the bearded man yelled as he shoved him down the stairs.

Behind them something detonated with a heart-stopping thud. Then there was a roar like nothing he had ever heard and searing heat.

Behdin leaped through a doorway on the next level and scrambled behind a wall. Intense heat blasted past him as he protected his face with the scarf he had been issued.

When the inferno had passed he searched for the man who had saved him. The bearded smoker was nowhere to be seen. A moment later he found what was left of him. His charred body lay smoldering on the stairs, the stench of burning flesh and hair thick in the air. The black vest was the only part of him unscathed by the flame.

Behdin staggered clear, doubled over and vomited on his boots. When he recovered he slumped against a wall and sobbed. There was no way he could survive and get Xeyal home. His little sister would die alone in the ruined city of Homs, far from her family and friends.

Wilda noted the loss of the drone as she moved through the remains of a department store on the street opposite her target building. She replayed the last few seconds of recorded footage and spotted a face behind the barrel of an AK-47. Freezing the image she studied the attacker's features. The boy looked young, and scared. Synthetic targets were always expressionless. What was he doing in a Sakkin training scenario? She knew they used live human targets, but she had assumed they were captured combatants or at least adults.

She paused behind a concrete wall and waited for the

others to get into position, tracking their movement on the map displayed on her HUD.

"Eight Two, attack now and create a diversion," ordered the squad leader.

Her railer powered up with a whine and she checked that her non-lethal systems, pulsar emitter and smoke grenades, were ready. Then she took a deep breath and moved out from cover.

Rounds struck her armor before she had taken a single step. The targeting system identified the shooters in the bottom level of the structure directly ahead and from the building the others were attacking. An explosion lifted her from the ground as a rocket detonated on the street. She landed heavily, her railer spitting tungsten penetrators as she dove sideways to avoid more explosions.

"Good diversion," said Tree with a chuckle over the comms network.

"Keep the chatter down," barked Seven Nine Nine.

Wilda charged forward and smashed her way through a wall. She caught a glimpse of a dark figure and fired twice. Her rounds found their target and a mechop exploded in a shower of sparks and hydraulic fluid.

A second robot launched itself at her, hitting her around the torso and driving her sideways against a wall.

Wilda's HUD flickered and went blank, but the suit's hydraulics remained online. She slammed her elbow into the top of the mechop's head then grasped it by the torso before driving her armor-encased knee into its chest.

She knew from previous experience that the mechops had limited unarmed combat capability. Their signature move was the lunge followed by a series of hammer punches designed to crush an enemy combatant. It was effective against an unarmored hostile but not a Sakkin operative wearing a berserker suit.

Blocking the volley of blows she kicked the robot in the center of the chest, sending it flying backward. As it slammed into the ground she leaped into the air and landed with both feet on its head.

The armored metal was not strong enough to resist the five hundred pound weight of her and the suit. It collapsed like a soda can, crushing the delicate circuitry inside.

As she stepped off the robot's head her sensors came back online and the HUD flickered to life.

"Eight Two, you dropped offline, report," transmitted the squad leader.

"Two mechops destroyed. Systems are rebooting." She suddenly realized that the damage gave her a unique opportunity. Releasing one hand from the suit's gauntlet she pulled her flexipad from one of the pouches on her chest. A bullet had nicked the plastic, but it still functioned. Using the access Henry had given her she hacked the suit and disabled the self-diagnosis and repair software. Then she checked to make sure her camera and tracking functionality was off.

"Eight Two, report."

She smiled. Their team leader sounded stressed. "Sorry, my systems have been damaged. I will continue clearing the objective. I can see your location but my transponder isn't working. I'm moving to the second floor of the target."

There was a pause as Seven Nine Nine processed the information. Wilda could hear gunfire from the opposite side of the street. Hopefully the others would be too preoccupied with their own fight to be concerned with her. She held her breath as she waited for a response.

"Keep me informed."

Wilda exhaled and returned the flexipad to her pouch. At least now she would not have big brother peering over her shoulder.

The Institute, Jordan

Marnisha frowned at the battle-tracking map displayed on the wall of the operations room. "What happened to Eight Two? I can't see her icon anymore."

She looked at the touch screen in front of her and stabbed Eight Two's symbol with her finger. A menu flashed up and she selected the live camera feed. It was grayed out.

"Ma'am," reported one of the staff. "Eight Two has sustained damage to her suit. Her feed and transponder are offline."

She turned to where Leon sat in his command chair. "Is she injured?"

He shrugged. "I've got a battle to run. The status of a single nonperforming trainee is not my priority." He gestured to one of his other staff members. "How many of the OFTs remain active on the primary target?"

"Eight, squad *Gurion* is decimating them."

"We may have to add some additional firepower to the hostile element."

Marnisha pursed her lips and turned her attention back to the central monitor. "If someone doesn't give me a status report on Eight Two I'm going to terminate the entire activity."

Leon snapped his fingers. "Give her what she wants."

The operations officer brought Eight Two's data card up on the main screen. A series of icons denoted the status of her weapons, communications equipment, armor and health.

"Her heart rate is elevated, but apart from that, her vital signs are strong," said the officer. "However, the data feed has a little over thirty seconds delay. If she's already dead we won't know for half a minute."

She gestured to the camera feeds being streamed from the other trainees. "So this is all a delayed broadcast?"

"Correct."

"Doesn't that make it a little hard to coordinate?"

Leon nodded. "It certainly does, which is why it takes skill to ensure the training objectives are met. Now that you've checked on your little pet, can I please have my battle map back?"

"By all means."

The main screen changed from Eight Two's data to a detailed 3D map of Homs. Icons indicated the location of squad *Gurion*'s members and the remaining OFTs.

"They're cutting through them too quickly. Bring a devastator in from the garage. Let's see how they deal with that."

"What is a devastator?" asked Marnisha.

He gestured to one of the side screens. "That is a devastator."

She turned to the screen where a 3D model of a tank spun slowly. The armored hulk sported a turret bristling with barrels and sensors. As far as Marnisha was concerned it looked like a piece of agricultural equipment. "What makes it so... devastating?"

"Are you kidding? It's got four thirty millimeter autocannons, elevation of sixty degrees, two automatic grenade launchers and one of the most sophisticated fire control systems available. Its liquid ferrous armor is specifically designed to defeat their railers and plasma rockets, so they'll have to get creative to withdraw intact. Trust me, this thing will shake them up."

Homs, Syria

Behdin felt the building tremble beneath him as explosions sounded from across the street. Gunfire echoed through the structure as he sat clutching his battered AK.

Four floors below, six black-vested prisoners were attempting to defend the building. Behdin was torn between going to help them and hiding. Not because he was afraid to make a stand and die, but because he needed to stay alive, so he could find his sister.

Another explosion detonated from across the street and he climbed to his feet. His father would never have deserted the fight; he was a man of honor, a warrior who would take a stand.

He carried his AK to the dark stairwell and descended to the next level. Below he could hear the shouts of the defenders. It sounded as if they were heading up toward him.

Another explosion rocked the building and footsteps rang on the stairs. Two men appeared, their eyes wide with terror.

"They hit us from the other building, fired rockets that burned everyone!" The two men ran past, continuing up the stairs. Behdin glanced below and heard something moving. "Wait for me!" he yelled as he turned to follow the others.

Suddenly an explosion thundered above along with a

flash of flame. He heard the cries of the other men as another of the fire rockets incinerated them. He stood transfixed as scorched air blasted his face, singeing his hair and eyebrows.

When the roar subsided all he could hear was the clump of the heavy footfalls below. Racking the action of the AK he checked to see a round was chambered. If he was going to die then he would go down fighting. It was what his father would do.

Wilda stood over the charred corpses of three men and swallowed the bile in her throat. The rest of the squad had launched plasma rockets from the building opposite, incinerating them. All that remained were rudimentary weapons, the vests they wore and their smoldering bodies.

She knelt alongside one and examined the vest. Despite the intense heat of the plasma warhead it was still intact. She prodded it with the berserker suit's gauntlet. She guessed this was how they were controlling the men.

"Eight Two, report your location," transmitted Seven Nine Nine.

"I'm on the second floor of my allocated target."

"Nice of you to join the fight. We just toasted the third floor. Keep climbing and neutralize what's left."

Wilda clenched her jaw as she moved toward the staircase. The squad had been firing at anything that moved. It did not seem to matter that the targets were now real people and not robots.

"I'm moving through to the fifth floor. Please refrain from tossing any more plasma in my direction."

"Then, I suggest you clear your objective," he snapped in reply.

Wilda reached the staircase and climbed as fast as the suit would allow. Cresting the landing she spotted movement to her right. Before she could react bullets slammed into her armor.

Spinning she aimed her railer at the assailant and found herself staring into the terrified face of a young boy. He was the same one she'd seen shoot the drone. More rounds ricocheted off her armor before his AK ran dry. The boy dropped the empty magazine and fumbled for another.

"Drop the gun!" yelled Wilda in Arabic.

The boy's hands shook as he struggled to fit the magazine. She had to act. At close range, there was a chance one of his bullets would find a weak spot in her armor.

"Activate pulse."

The boy rammed the magazine home and wrenched the cocking handle back as Wilda aimed the forearm-mounted emitter. She fired as he raised the assault rifle.

A ball of static charged energy slammed into his frame, throwing him against the wall. His head smacked into the concrete then he dropped to the floor in a heap.

"I've killed him," murmured Wilda as she moved to his side and knelt. The medical scanner attached to her gauntlet indicated that he was unconscious, but breathing. As she turned him into the recovery position she noticed that, beneath old canvas ammunition pouches, he wore the same black vest she had seen on the others. Closer inspection revealed that it had an electronic module attached to it that included a speaker and an antenna.

She straightened and released her arms from the exoskeleton so she could use her flexipad. In a matter of seconds she found the vest's signal and a dozen more like it.

A quick scan though the code confirmed her suspicions. The vest contained heart rate monitoring technology, a kill charge, tracking software and a long-range radio. It effectively turned the wearer into a radio-controlled drone. Sakkin was using the devices to force innocent people to fight.

As she delved into the code her radio hissed. "Eight Two, objective is secured. We're moving back to the ground level."

"Acknowledged, I'll be clear here in a minute. I'll meet you there."

She hurriedly hacked the vest and searched for a way to deactivate it. The key was giving the impression the boy had been killed and the vest destroyed.

As she scrolled through the lines of code she found something that made her physically ill. A command line fired the explosive charge if the vest was unable to connect to the Sakkin network for a period of more than two hours. It did not matter how hard the boy fought, he was destined to die.

"Not on my watch." She deleted the line and deactivated the charge. Stowing her flexipad she drew the combat knife from its forearm sheath and used it to cut the lethal vest from the boy.

Seven Nine Nine prodded a corpse with his boot as he waited for the rest of squad *Gurion* to gather on the bottom floor. There had been a dozen hostiles inside the building armed with a variety of antiquated weapons. Under his direction the squad had made short work of them. The rooms and corridors were littered with corpses blown apart by railers or toasted by plasma rockets and grenades.

He grinned inside his helmet as he crushed the charred skull under the berserker suit's carbon fiber boot. The mission had been a success and he was one step closer to graduating from the *Institute*. The only thing that could improve his day would be Eight Two being killed by one of the hostiles.

"We've got movement up the street," said Tree from where he stood in the doorway of the building.

Seven Nine Nine scraped the brains from his boot and strode toward him. "What is—"

A massive blast knocked Tree over. Then a stream of high explosive rounds lashed the building. Shrapnel, dust and chips of concrete ricocheted from Seven Nine Nine's armor as automatic cannon fire raked the walls. "Fall back!" he screamed, grabbing Tree's berserker suit and dragging him clear.

Rounds pulverized the entire frontage of the building.

"It's a god damn devastator!" screamed Tree as Seven Nine dragged him deeper into the building.

The other trainees stood bewildered as more explosions rocked the room. There was an almighty roar and fire engulfed them. Despite their fire retardant heavy armor the heat was oppressive.

When the flames subsided Seven Nine Nine checked his team.

Tree's suit had been critically damaged, but he was unharmed. The others were only scorched.

"That thing will cut us to shreds!" yelled Tree as he lay on the ground, struggling with his suit's emergency release.

On cue, a volley of armor piercing rounds smashed through the wall sending the team diving to the ground.

"We need to get out of here," said one of the squad members.

Tree finally managed to extricate himself from his suit. "Where the hell is Eight Two?"

"With any luck she's dead," replied Seven Nine Nine as he crawled toward the room's only exit.

Wilda was far from dead. She had heard the cannon fire from the street and rushed to the side of the building. She spotted the devastator as it unleashed a volley of high explosive rounds, blowing jagged holes in the walls.

She smirked as she checked her battle map. Seven Nine Nine and his team of killers were getting exactly what they deserved. The tank had them pinned in the lower level of the target building.

As she watched, a huge chunk of the second floor collapsed, throwing a cloud of dust into the street. Railer projectiles punched out and flashed against the hundred ton behemoth's body. She knew from previous briefings that the railers were unlikely to penetrate the liquid ferrous armor that encased the massive war machine.

Sure enough the devastator continued its unrelenting bombardment of the team's position. As the smell of high explosive wafted in through the vents of her helmet Wilda realized she had to do something. If Seven Nine Nine or any of the others were killed then the mission would be a failure and the remaining trainees would not graduate. That would significantly impede her ability to find the truth about where she had come from and what Sakkin had done to her mother.

One option was to engage the devastator at close range with plasma or explosive charges, a risky tactic. However, if she could get close enough, she might be able to use the flexipad to hack its system and override the controls.

Below her, the tank rumbled along the street, moving into a better position to attack the target building. Wilda eyed the growing gap between her and the multi-barreled turret. In a matter of seconds it would be out of range.

Backing up she grit her teeth and sprinted forward. The suit accelerated her to sixty miles an hour and then she was airborne.

Her scream filled her helmet as she sailed through the air, arms and legs flailing. Then she hit the side of the turret with an almighty clang. She almost bounced off, but managed to grab a smoking barrel with one gauntlet.

The turret spun wildly as she clung to it. The system had detected her presence and tried to shake her loose. As it rotated she released an arm from the suit's gauntlet and slid the flexipad from its pouch. With her suit clamped to the devastator she managed to free both hands and activate the device. It took her a moment to find the tank's interface and a few more seconds to hack into it.

Scanning line after line of code she finally found what she was looking for; a shutdown order. As she was about to activate it the berserker suit's grip on the barrel slipped and the flexipad dropped from her hands and bounced onto the sand-covered street.

She reached up to her shoulder and yanked the berserker suit's emergency release.

The exoskeleton and helmet fell off her in pieces and she was flung from the tank in only her underarmor and combat boots. She heard the turret spin toward her as she dove for the flexipad. A cannon roared and rounds ripped over her head as she traced her fingers over the damaged device.

The tank could not depress its guns low enough to hit her. Instead it rumbled forward in an attempt to crush her. The tracks rattled and squeaked as it rolled forward. It was a few feet away when she activated a command. For a moment she thought it had failed, but as she rolled sideways the devastator shuddered to a halt.

She scanned the lines of code then activated another command. A maintenance hatch on the rear of the tank popped open. She grabbed a plasma grenade from the chest piece of her dismantled berserker suit. Arming the delayed fuse she tossed it through the hatch and sprinted back toward the foyer of her building.

The tank exploded as she reached the building. Realizing the questions the flexipad would prompt she buried it in a pile of sand. She finished covering the device and glanced up at one of the buildings opposite. A frown formed on her face. She swore that for a split second a bearded face had watched her through a hole in the wall.

Heavy footfalls approached from behind and she turned to see the rest of squad *Gurion* emerging from the shattered building. She noted that Tree, like her, was missing his exoskeleton.

She rose from the ruins and waved her arms, before moving across to join them.

"Did you do that?" Tree asked, pointing at the smoldering remains of the tank.

She nodded.

He reached out and shook her hand. "You saved us."

The other members of the team gathered around her

and offered their own thanks. All except Seven Nine Nine, who glared at her. "Evac bird is inbound. We need to get to the landing zone in fifteen minutes." He pointed to Tree and Wilda. "And you two are going to slow us down. Get a move on."

Chapter Ten

Homs, Syria

As Wilda and her team extracted from the city Behdin moaned and attempted to sit upright. His entire body ached, his vision was blurry and he could taste the coppery flavor of blood in his mouth.

Then he remembered the camouflaged robot that had fired on him. It had caught him by surprise, the shimmering shape blending with the concrete walls and rubble. He scrabbled for his AK and found it a short distance away. He grabbed it with one hand feeling for the wall with the other. Struggling to his feet he dragged his sleeve across his eyes and listened.

Over the thump of his heart he could hear nothing other than the wind blowing through the building's open levels. Blinking rapidly he managed to clear his vision. Scanning his surroundings he found no sign of any of the mechanical killers. He moved tentatively through the building, crouched at a shattered window and checked the street.

Below, a massive tank burned and across the street smoke billowed from a collapsed shop front. Exhaling Behdin slumped against a concrete column, dropped his head into his hands and wept. For some reason he was still alive when everyone else had died. It was then that he realized he was no longer wearing the black vest. He looked around and saw it a few feet away, beside his chest rig.

A closer inspection revealed that the shoulder joints had been cut. Someone had freed him. He wiped the tears from his eyes and checked the magazine on his AK. It was still full. Now, without the vest, the odds of rescuing Xeyal had increased.

He shrugged into his chest rig and made his way back to the stairs before climbing toward the roof. On the next level he found the charred remains of the other men. He wound his headscarf around his face to block the stench and continued upward.

Three stories later he stood atop the building, searching for a landmark that would lead him to the prison. There, a few blocks away he could see a tall metal tower. He remembered seeing it from the truck.

Fueled by hope he jogged downstairs, past the carnage of the gunfight and out onto the street. As he ran past the smoldering tank he stopped, spotting something on the ground. Brushing sand aside he uncovered a thin clear device. He picked it up and the flexible screen glowed, then transformed into some kind of tablet computer with words and pictures.

As he examined the tablet he heard a clatter from the building opposite. He stuffed the device in his shirt and snatched up his AK, scrambling behind a pillar as a figure left the building. Peering around he saw two more men, all carrying weapons. Clad in a motley array of fatigues with scarves around their faces, they inspected the wrecked tank.

"Drop the gun."

The man's voice came from behind. He lowered the AK to the ground.

"Turn around, slowly."

Behdin complied and found himself looking down the barrel of a pistol.

The man's face was wrapped in a swath of grubby checkered cloth. His eyes were dark and intelligent, the whites tinged with red from the desert sand. He carried a faded green satchel over a threadbare khaki shirt.

"No enslaving vest," he said. "Where did you come from, boy?"

"I had a vest. It's back in the building."

The man pulled aside the cloth, revealing features aged by the desert sun. He had a bulbous nose and a broad mouth surrounded by a patchy beard. "You had a vest? How did you take it off?"

Behdin shrugged. "One of the robots knocked me out. When I woke, it was off."

Behind him, he heard a clanking sound. He glanced over his shoulder and saw one of the men attacking a destroyed robot with a wrench.

"They're not all robots," the man replied. "Some of them have people inside."

Suddenly a piercing whistle echoed off the concrete walls.

"Shit, they're coming." He ran past and called out to the others. "Times up, grab what you can!"

Turning he took Behdin by the arm. "We've got to go." He bent and grabbed the AK before leading him out of the building, across the street and under a faded sign with a picture of a man drinking from a can.

"Who is coming?" Behdin asked as they weaved through dust-covered shelves.

"The hunters come to clean up after the battle. If we hang around outside, they'll terminate us." He pushed open a steel door, pulled a glowing rod from his satchel and illuminated a flight of bare concrete stairs. "We'll be safe down here."

Behdin shook his head. "No, I need to stay on the surface. I have to get back to the prison."

The man shook his head. "Why the hell would you want to go there?"

He choked back tears as he turned to the man. "My sister is there. She's only twelve. They put a vest on her."

"They're animals. Look, we might be able to save your sister. If the others found what we need, then we might be able to rescue everyone."

Something about the man, perhaps the authority in his voice, reassured Behdin that he could be trusted. He nodded and followed him down the stairs into the basement. "What were you looking for?"

The man led him through a hole in a brick wall into a narrow corridor. "A power source."

"Like a battery?"

"Yes, except a battery powerful enough to run a city. Those ones are kind of hard to come by." The man stopped halfway along the walkway and pulled a metal bar out from behind the steel pipe that hung from the ceiling.

Behdin watched as he used it to pry a thick steel plate from the floor.

"What's your name?" he grunted as he shifted it.

"Behdin."

He replaced the bar and gestured to the open hole. "My name is Hanan. Welcome to the underground."

The Institute, Jordan

Wilda stepped off the ramp of the MX22 and glanced at the massive hangar doors above. Beyond them, an ominous shape hovered in the sky. The cigar-shaped object was one of Sakkin's aerostats. She had spotted the airship through the window of the vertjet as they flew in.

"Debriefing in room five," ordered the black-clad Sakkin operative waiting a few feet away.

She felt naked without the exoskeleton as she left the hangar and walked through the armory. The others clumped their way to the bays to stow their berserker suits as she and Tree waited opposite the workshop.

She had hoped to see Henry working diligently, but his space was dark and empty.

"Pretty impressive," said Tree, breaking the silence.

"Huh?" she turned to face him.

"I've never heard of a trainee destroying a devastator before. How did you do it?"

She shrugged. "For some reason the maintenance hatch was open. I tossed a plasma grenade in and waited for the fireworks." Turning to the workshop she wondered where Henry had gone. She glanced toward the racks where the berserker suits and mechops were kept. Perhaps he was out back working on a faulty piece of equipment.

When the rest of the team assembled Seven Nine Nine led them into an elevator and up to the briefing rooms where they sat in front of a bank of screens.

A computer program took them through each step of the mission. Because of the modifications she'd made to her berserker suit her efforts were absent from the analysis. However, she did get to relive the death of every one of the 'hostiles' that her teammates had murdered. The program treated them as inanimate objects, cogs in the Sakkin machine. It made her sick to watch Seven Nine Nine and the others revel in each kill. She took some solace in knowing that she had saved a young boy from certain death.

When they reached the phase in the battle where the devastator had appeared the program attributed the kill to a maintenance issue. Tree tried to enlighten the process with a version of the truth but Seven Nine Nine cut him off.

Wilda was happy with that. Battle damage and a maintenance issue were exactly what she wanted the Sakkin software and hierarchy to believe.

She yawned as the debrief concluded and the team made their way out of the room. She looked forward to some rest.

However, as they reached the elevator one of the Sakkin instructors stopped them. "Squad *Gurion* is to report immediately to the hangar."

They let out a collective groan.

"Do we have time to get cleaned up?" asked Wilda.

"What part of immediately is unclear to you?"

They entered the elevator and when the doors slammed shut Seven Nine Nine turned to her. "Learn to keep your mouth shut, Eight Two. I don't need you drawing attention to us."

"But, feel free to draw heat away from us," added one of the other team members. "That move with the devastator was killer."

The squad leader silenced him with a glare as they reached the armory and flight deck level.

As they walked past the workshop there was still no sign of Henry. She glanced into the mechop bays, but he was not there either.

"What are you looking for?" asked Tree as they reached the landing pad.

"What? Nothing." Wilda glanced back over her shoulder as another Sakkin operative waved the team inside a waiting vertjet.

Homs, Syria

Behdin had lost all sense of direction as he followed Hanan through a labyrinth of tunnels. In his mind they were traveling deeper and deeper beneath the ruined city.

He wound his scarf tighter around his neck as they crouched to enter a narrow tunnel. It was far cooler underground than in the blistering sun.

Finally, they emerged from the tight tunnel into a large cellar with a high arched ceiling lit by electric lamps. Eight men sat around a long table piled with weapons, cans of food and equipment.

Glancing around the room he saw that there were bunks on one side. The other walls were stacked high with boxes and military hardware.

"My friends, this is Behdin," announced Hanan as he hung his satchel on the back of a chair.

The other men in the room acknowledged him with nods and greetings in a number of dialects.

"How did we go?" Hanan took a seat at the head of the table and gestured for Behdin to join them.

A man with a lean face, gray beard and squinty eyes shook his head as he tossed a component on the table. "No good. We need an ultracapacitor." He turned and stared at Behdin. "Where did he come from?"

"He was a drone, but somehow his enslaving vest was removed."

The others stopped what they were doing and all heads turned to Behdin.

"That's never happened before," said the man. "How do you know he's not a spy?"

"I'm not a spy!" yelled Behdin. "My sister is in the prison. They put a vest on both of us."

"Calm down, boy," said Hanan. "Listen, there's no chance the kid works for Sakkin, which means he's with us now. Right?" He looked each of them in the eye.

The eight men stayed silent and Hanan continued, "He's the only one who's been to the prison. We'll need him later. Now, did we get anything useful?"

"A couple of AKs and a rocket launcher," replied another of the men. "That and a bunch of trash. There was an exoskeleton near the tank, but I couldn't move it in time."

"There will be another mission soon and another opportunity."

Behdin reached into his jacket and removed the flexipad. He handed it to Hanan. "I found this."

"Is that a flexipad? Give it to me," demanded the man with the squinty eyes.

"Eon was a scientist with Sakkin," explained Hanan as he handed it over.

"Until they decided to test my equipment on living

people," he said as he took a pair of worn spectacles from his pocket and examined the flexipad. He placed his finger on the screen then shook it before tossing the device on the table. "Without a logon it is useless. Hanan, we need an ultracapacitor. Without it the CHAMP won't work."

"I know. We'll get one eventually."

"What about my sister?" demanded Behdin.

Hanan placed his hand on the boy's shoulder. "Of course. We'll do everything we can to rescue her. But now you need to rest and eat."

Behdin nodded as he reached across the table for the flexipad. One of the other men placed a hand on it.

The scientist shrugged. "Let the boy have it. It's worthless."

They let him take the flexipad and he followed Hanan across to the corner of the room. "Is it true? What he said?"

"What was that?"

"That no one has gotten out of a vest before?"

"As far as I'm aware. You have no idea how yours came off, do you?"

Behdin shook his head.

"Look, the enslaving vests can malfunction, they can be destroyed," Hanan continued. "With what we've got planned, we may just be able to help everyone with them, including your sister." He handed him an energy bar.

Behdin unwrapped the snack and sniffed it. The dull gray substance hardly smelled edible.

"It's safe to eat." He directed Behdin to a bunk. "Get some rest. Then we can talk more about your sister."

He sat on the bed and held the bar in his hand as he watched the men sorting through the items on the table. He had no appetite. All he could think about was Xeyal, alone and terrified. One way or another, he would rescue her.

Shadow Runner, Jordan

Henry was still on Wilda's mind as she stepped out of the vertjet into the hold of what she assumed was the aerostat she had seen above the *Institute*. A quick survey of the compact space confirmed her assessment.

One side of the Sakkin airship's hangar was lined with the latest generation of clankers. Their limp black bodies hung like deadly dolls from a dispersal rack. On the opposite side a similar configuration held more than a dozen of the disc-shaped hunter drones and six berserker suits.

A black-uniformed man met them at the entrance to the hangar. "Welcome aboard the aerostat *Shadow Runner*. Follow me." He led the team into a bare aluminum-walled room the size of a shipping container. There was a briefing screen at one end and fold down bunks on either side. "This is your ready room. You'll be briefed within the hour. Seven Nine Nine, you're to accompany me to the command center."

"Looks like we're on our next mission," said Tree as their squad leader departed.

"We're going back to Homs?" asked one of the others.

"That would be my guess. What about you, Eight Two?" said Tree.

She frowned. "What?"

"Dreaming again?"

"Just thinking about the next mission." She sat on one of the bunks.

Tree nodded. "This one's going to be harder. But, at least we know you can take care of any devastators."

Wilda grimaced, without her flexipad she had lost the

ability to back-door Sakkin's systems. She'd hoped she could get another one from Henry, but now it seemed that something had happened to her only friend.

As team *Gurion* made themselves comfortable Leon Wilken stood in a classic soldier's parade ground rest position looking out from the observation deck of the aerostat. Hands clasped in the small of his back he studied the desert below as the autopilot guided them toward a cruising altitude of thirty thousand feet.

He felt almost godlike, looking down on the world below and knowing the firepower that he had at his fingertips. *Shadow Runner* was one of the smaller craft in the Sakkin fleet, but even so, it sported a deadly arsenal of mechops, drones, precision-guided bombs, close defense lasers and of course, trainee ganic operatives.

"Sir," a voice called from behind. "Dr. Copeland is requesting transfer from the *Institute*."

Leon turned and strode across to the operations table, a glass digital map in the center of the control room. Two of his officers stood over it coordinating the aircraft's movement and preparations for the training activity through their wireless headsets.

He had hoped Marnisha would have lost interest in the *Tsalmaveth* and returned to Sakkin HQ, where she belonged. "Send the vertjet. Let me know when she's aboard."

"Yes, sir."

The door to the bridge hissed open and Shona entered. In her tight-fitting uniform the attractive blond was a distraction he didn't need. "Marnisha is coming aboard. You'll have to make yourself scarce."

She scowled. "Seriously, that bitch is getting on my nerves."

He sighed. "Mine too. Is everything ready from your end?"

She nodded.

"You're sure Eight Two can't weasel her way out of this?"

"No. She'll never complete the mission and then you can terminate her." She grinned. "And then Lisker will see what a failure Marnisha's work has been and fire her."

Leon nodded as the door opened and one of his staff escorted Seven Nine Nine in.

The senior trainee spotted the officer and braced with his fists pressed against his thighs.

"Seven Nine Nine, so far your team's performance in the *Tsalmaveth* has been assessed as poor."

He saw a flash of anger in the young man's eyes.

"One of your team members," he continued, "has been identified as the primary reason for this assessment. Trainee Eight Two has failed to follow orders and endangered your entire team."

The squad leader's chin dipped every so slightly in agreement.

"I have reason to doubt her loyalty to *Gurion* and to Sakkin. Which is why we've placed something in your next mission specifically to test her. If she fails, I want you to terminate her."

The trainee's brow rose, then he quickly composed himself. "Yes, sir. May I ask what the test is?"

"You're to assign her the task of neutralizing the high-value target on the next mission. If she fails, you make sure she does not return. Do you understand?"

"Yes, sir."

"Good." He dismissed the man with a wave of his hand. A waiting staff member directed the trainee out of the room.

"You sure all the arrangements have been made?" Leon asked when he was gone.

"Yes," replied Shona. "Everything is in place."

"Good, now get out of here before Marnisha arrives. The last thing I need is you antagonizing her before the mission begins."

She glared at him before turning on her heel and storming out of the room. He grimaced; no doubt, he would wear the consequences of her rage later. He turned his attention back to the windows and the shrinking desert below.

"Sir, Doctor Copeland's vertjet has docked," one of the officers announced.

"Good, commence transit to the Homs training area."

"Aye, sir. Transit time estimated at six hours and thirty minutes."

The deck trembled under his boots as the thrusters increased their output and the aerostat gained momentum. He had worked from the earlier models of the airships. Far more spartan in their layout they had been used as mobile operating bases from which Sakkin forces had struck at terrorist cells across the globe. With the loss of satellites they were vital in providing communications, intelligence and firepower to support the small but lethal ground teams out hunting prey.

Flying at thirty thousand feet they were far beyond the range of machine guns and anti-aircraft cannons. Despite its slow speed and hulking size, the craft was also impervious to missiles and fighter jets. An array of sensors and lasers could detect and engage hundreds of targets simultaneously.

He had been on one at the height of the Greater Middle Eastern Conflict that had destroyed over fifty Surface to Air Missiles in a four hour period. Leon grinned. He and his mechops had been sent out to destroy the launch sites that night. Once they'd landed on the ground it had been a massacre.

He heard the door hiss open and turned to see Marnisha entering. Her heels rang on the aluminum floor as she strode toward him in a business suit. "Welcome aboard, Doctor."

"Thank you, Leon." She glanced around the cabin. "I expected it to be a little larger." A smile broke her icy demeanor. "But, you'd be used to hearing that. How long till we reach the objective?"

He glared at her. "A little over six hours."

"And the trainees are onboard?" She took a seat at the operations table and folded her hands in her lap.

"Yes, all arrangements are in place. My staff will show you to your cabin."

"That can wait. First, I want you to take me through the training mission."

"Of course," he said tersely. As he leaned over the digital map and activated the mission master template he could not help but smirk. He was going to savor the moment when she watched her project go up in flames.

Chapter Eleven

Homs, Syria

Xeyal wept as she cowered in the bed of a truck rattling through the streets of a devastated city. Like her brother she had been ordered through the gate, armed and loaded for transport.

There had been no sign of Hanan among the other prisoners in the truck. None of them had any idea what had happened to those that had left first.

She glanced around at the faces of her companions. They clutched their weapons with white-knuckled hands, faces pale and eyes wide. It did nothing to alleviate the terror she felt.

Outside all she saw was an empty city ravaged by warfare. Buildings with their walls crumbled showed their innards to the world. To Xeyal they resembled the bones of long-dead monsters.

She struggled to carry the heavy AK assault rifle as she followed the others from the back of the truck. Sinister black robots herded them into an open square surrounded on all sides by tall buildings. The structures were like nothing she had ever seen before, reaching far into the sky. The damage here was not as extensive as the rest of the city. Shell holes pockmarked the buildings, but their walls were intact.

As Xeyal stood at the edge of the group she clutched the AK and wept. Little did she know that friendly eyes watched them.

Eight hundred yards from the edge of Al-Baath University, in the ruins of a heavily shelled shop, Hanan looked through a spotting scope, his filthy robe blending with the debris and dust. Behind him sat Behdin, crouched in the mouth of a narrow tunnel with his AK cradled in his lap.

"Can you see her?" the boy whispered.

"There are thirty or more people in the square. It's hard to identify an individual."

The boy slid out of the tunnel and crawled up alongside him. "Can I look?"

Hanan handed over the scope.

Behdin held it to his eye, adjusting the focal point so he could see clearly.

Like Hanan had said there was a large group of people in the square. They all carried weapons and wore the black vests that condemned them to death.

As he scanned the group, his heart skipped a beat. There was a small figure at the edge of the crowd. He adjusted the zoom until he could make out the shape. It was a small girl with dark brown hair. "She's still alive," he murmured, lowering the scope. "We need to get her out."

Hanan placed a hand on his shoulder. "In due course. First, we need to get our people into position." He slid back into the tunnel.

Behdin took one last look at his sister. "I'm going to rescue you Xeyal. I promise."

Shadow Runner, Syria

Wilda lay on one of the top bunks in the ready room staring at the ceiling. For the past six hours she had laid on the hard mattress worrying about Henry. It was unusual for him to be away from the workshop. Had there been a medical emergency? Was he in some sort of trouble for helping her? There was no way she could find out without compromising their relationship. Exhaling she tried to push him from her mind. Stressing about Henry would not help her solve the short-term problem.

She needed to find a way out of the *Tsalmaveth*. Without Henry's help and her flexipad there was no way she could avoid taking an innocent life. There was every chance this mission would be her last. Turning to face the wall she slid her notebook from the pocket of her uniform. Flicking through the pages she came to the sketch of her mother. "What would you do?" she murmured.

An alarm sounded and she stuffed the notebook into her pocket as the other trainees rose from their bunks. Lowering to the floor she joined them in the center of the room.

"What does that mean?" asked Tree.

"It means we've reached our infil point," barked Seven Nine Nine from where he lay on a bunk. Wilda watched as the squad leader sat up and swung his legs out onto the floor. "It means soon we will complete the final phase of the *Tsalmaveth*." He looked Wilda directly in the eye. "Well, maybe not all of us."

He rose from the bed. "We've been tasked with a kill mission; there will be an intelligence briefing in the next fifteen minutes. I suggest you all grab something to eat from the galley and check your equipment."

As her team members leaped into action Wilda felt a sense of foreboding. She waited for Seven Nine Nine to issue another threat, but instead, he smiled at her as he passed and left the room. The look left her feeling sick with anxiety. Something was going on and she had no idea what it was.

"He really doesn't like you," said Tree, the only trainee left in the room.

She managed a chuckle. "Neither do you."

"Yeah, but I respect your skill. Good luck out there." He left Wilda alone in the room.

Despite Tree's words she still felt an overwhelming hopelessness. She was alone in her fight and there was every chance that she would not succeed.

Homs, Syria

Behdin sat in a dark corner of the cellar listening to the men of the underground. Their discussion was heated, arguing over their options for securing the equipment they needed. As he sat he fidgeted with a flashlight and the spotting scope that Hanan had given him. He stowed them in his chest rig, along with the remaining magazines for his AK and the cracked flexipad.

"It is pointless trying to rescue any of them at this stage," announced one of the men. He gestured to a stack of tubes in the corner of the room. "We've got next to no plasma rockets. We shoot our wad to rescue prisoners and we have zero hope of getting a power source. We need to set up an ambush and target a single clanker."

Light from the lanterns cast dark shadows on the men's faces.

"What about the boy?" said Hanan. "Somehow his vest was removed."

"How do we know if he ever had one on?" the man snapped.

"The risk is too great, Hanan." This time it was Eon, the scientist, who spoke. "Nathan is right. Our only hope is to recover a power source for the missile. Then, and only then do we have a chance of rescuing the drones. If we expose ourselves before that there is no hope, for anyone."

Behdin waited for Hanan's response. When the leader said nothing, he realized no one was going to help him save his sister. Quietly he gathered his AK and slipped out into a tunnel.

As he stole away from the men he could hear their voices echoing. He had no more interest in what they had to say. Hanan and the others had proven themselves to be all talk and no action. There was only one person who could save Xeyal.

The tunnel ran a hundred yards before he found an exit that emerged into the ruins of an apartment block. He scrambled through the shattered building, climbing slabs of concrete and piles of rubble until he reached what remained of the upper level.

Hiding under a sheet of iron he took the scope from his vest and peered through it. The place where he had seen Xeyal was at least three fields distant. There were a dozen of the black robots standing in a circle, but the prisoners were gone. He needed to get closer.

Using the scope he planned a route through the ruined buildings that would hide him from the robots.

A faint roaring noise to the west caught his attention and he glanced toward the horizon. Light reflected from something in the distance. The object rapidly grew in size until he could identify it as one of the flying machines that attacked his village.

The craft landed in the center of the circle of robots and a ramp lowered. More dark figures appeared and he refocused the scope. One of them seemed to be carrying a hooded figure in its arms. Another prisoner brought to die with the others, he thought as he picked up his AK. Sliding down an angled wall he hit the ground running. Something told him he needed to move fast if he was going to save Xeyal.

Chapter Twelve

Homs, Syria

Wilda's heart raced as she stood at the edge of the aerostat's open hangar floor clad in the latest generation of jumper suit. This model included enhanced ballistic protection and had the same adaptive camouflage as the berserkers. A module on her back contained the carbon-weave chute that would arrest her fall. Her railer was clipped to her right leg and an array of pouches contained grenades and other equipment.

"Standby," ordered Seven Nine Nine over the comms channel.

She glanced sideways as her teammates lined up alongside her. Equipped with the jumper suits squad *Gurion* looked formidable. With their faces hidden by their helmets they were robotic killers, not free-willed teenagers. For a split second Wilda's sorrow overcame the anticipation of freefall.

"Go."

Wilda stepped forward. Her stomach lurched as she dropped like a rock through a haze- filled sky. The exhilaration of falling blew away her sorrow as she used the suit's control surfaces to level her flight.

The HUD inside her helmet displayed 3D gateways. Passing through them ensured she was on track with the rest of the team. It was a short freefall before her suit activated the canopy then guided her over the ruined city of Homs.

Squad Gurion touched down simultaneously, landing in a dusty sports field surrounded by derelict apartment blocks. Their black chutes detached and the wind dragged them away, leaving their adaptive camouflage to blend with the drab urban terrain.

Wilda scanned the buildings that towered on either side. Her sensors failed to pick up any sign of life. In accordance with the plan that Seven Nine Nine had briefed earlier they'd landed a half-mile from their objective.

Their target, a terrorist cell leader, had been staging his attacks from within Al-Baath University. Intelligence had identified his headquarters inside a building at the center, and Seven Nine Nine had planned a covered approach route. He had deviated from his standard operating procedure by putting Tree on point. Wilda was thankful for minor wins, moving further back in the team meant she was unlikely to be the first to fire. She could still find a way to avoid killing innocents.

She fell into place as the team moved off in single file. Tree led them at a steady pace, patrolling with their railers held ready. According to the intelligence file the battered remains of the university had once housed forty thousand students. She glanced around at the crumbling concrete and skeletal structures. It felt more like a tomb than an education facility. It was in slightly better condition than the rest of the city but still showed the scars of decades of conflict.

The team wove its way through a gutted building and reached the outer edge of the accommodation sector. Wilda crouched behind a wall, scanning the open terrain to their front. What had once been a lush green park was now a cratered moonscape.

"Eight Two, you and Tree scout ahead. The rest of us will cover you," transmitted Seven Nine Nine.

Wilda rolled her eyes. Their squad leader was so predictable. Tree had shown her a small amount of respect and now Seven Nine Nine was punishing them both.

A flashing symbol on her HUD told her Tree had opened a private channel between the two of them. "Let's do this. Standard leapfrog, right?"

"Yeah, I'll go first." Wilda checked her adaptive camouflage was active then moved swiftly from behind cover.

Rocks crunched under the suit's boots as she ran for a crater. She slid into it and knelt. A moment later the camouflaged form of Tree arrived alongside.

"I'll take the next leg," he said.

"Covering."

Tree dashed across the clearing toward the buildings on the far side. He was almost there when a half-dozen hostile target symbols flashed in Wilda's HUD.

Bullets struck the ground around him and his adaptive camouflage flickered as they hit his armor.

"Damn!" he bellowed as an explosion blasted him sideways.

Wilda's suit provided targeting solutions for all the points of origin, but she held her fire. Instead, she raised her arm and fired a volley of smoke grenades.

She heard the snap of railers and the roar of a plasma

rocket as the rest of the team unleashed. Her thermal sensors showed the impact, the upper part of a building opposite exploded outward, showering her with debris. Something landed alongside her with a soft thud. Dead eyes stared up from the smoldering corpse of a middle-aged man dressed in the same type of vest she had removed from the boy on their last mission.

"Eight Two, are you going to join me?" transmitted Tree from the building ahead.

Tearing her eyes from the body she dashed through the smoke to where he waited.

"Secure the building," ordered their squad leader as she ducked through a shell hole into a room. Shattered tables and twisted chairs indicated it had once been a classroom.

"They vaped the upper level," said Tree as he moved deeper into the building.

"I saw." Wilda followed him along a corridor and up a staircase.

On the top floor of the three-story building they found bodies smoldering among the rubble. All of them wore the same vest as the others.

"Seven Nine Nine, we're firm. You're free to move," reported Tree.

Wilda was glad he could not see the tears that spilled from her eyes behind her helmet's faceplate. The air filters scrubbed the stench of burning flesh from the air, but not her imagination. In her mind she could hear their screams echoing off the blackened walls as they writhed in agony.

"Good work," transmitted Seven Nine Nine. "That's how I like my hostiles, well done."

She turned to see the rest of the team emerge from the stairwell.

"Yeah, well there's more inbound," said Tree.

Rounds snapped through the air and an RPG detonated below them as an array of hostile indicators appeared in Wilda's HUD.

"Hostile clankers have got a bead on our location," said one of her squad mates.

"Good, we'll hold firm here while Eight Two flanks the compound and neutralizes the target," ordered Seven Nine Nine.

She frowned, why would he want her to carry out their mission alone?

"I'll go with her," added Tree.

"No, she goes alone." The squad leader moved to the edge of the building and fired three rounds from his railer.

Return fire slammed into the building as the others joined him. When they were all in position he turned and strode back to Wilda, stopping when their helmets almost touched. "I can't wait for you to fuck this up, because when you do, it's going to be the end of the road."

Shadow Runner, Syria

Marnisha frowned as she watched the interaction between the two trainees via the camera built into the squad leader's suit. She looked up at Leon, seated on the opposite side of the aerostat's operations table. "Why is he sending her in alone?"

The Head Instructor smirked. "Because I told him to. She did so well on the previous mission that I thought we should push her a little harder."

She fought the urge to berate the man in front of his subordinates. Instead, she nodded in agreement. "Good idea. I mean, your idiot of a squad leader has proven to have zero imagination. Perhaps Eight Two can add a little tactical flair to the operation."

Leon's eyes narrowed as he met her gaze. "Tactical flair is why missions fail. Seven Nine Nine is following standard procedures and…" He gestured to the hostile kill count displayed on the wall. It showed that over half the OFTs and a third of the mechops had been neutralized. "It seems to be working just fine."

Marnisha shrugged. "There are more important things than kill counts, Leon." Tasking Eight Two to operate independently did not overly concern the scientist; it was exactly the role that the trainee was destined to perform when she graduated from the *Institute*.

There was a hiss to her left as the door to the bridge opened. She glanced sideways and spotted Shona. Frowning she turned back to Leon.

"It is important for her to see this phase of the operation," he said. "She needs to evaluate the psychological profile of each of the team members."

Marnisha laughed. "You mean you need to assess how successful you've been in converting them into simple-minded killers?"

Leon snickered. "Come now, we've all played our part." He rose from his chair and leaned over the digital map. "Now," he said winking at Shona as she stood opposite. "Let's see how the mission pans out."

Homs, Syria

Behdin hugged the earth as hypervelocity penetrators drilled through the room. The projectiles blasted through reinforced concrete like it was plastic, showering him with dust and debris. The people in their robotic suits had started their assault and were systematically killing the other prisoners. He knew he was running out of time to find Xeyal.

There was a lull in the fire and he sprinted out of the room and along a narrow corridor. Finding a rusty metal ladder he climbed it to the floor above.

Upstairs he found a group of three men struggling to move a tripod-mounted rocket launcher, all wearing the black vests. One of them gestured for him to help. He did not recognize the harsh words that accompanied the request.

Another of the men studied him through shrewd eyes, then extended a bony finger and babbled excitedly. All three began scrutinizing him. Behdin adjusted his grip on the AK.

"You speak English?" asked the first man.

He nodded. "I'm looking for a young girl. She has green eyes and long brown hair."

"Why don't you have a vest?" asked boney finger.

"The girl. Have any of you seen my sister, Xeyal?"

"So you had a vest?" the man persisted.

Behdin scowled. "Yes, I had a vest. Now, have you seen her?"

"There was a girl in the other group. They're in the building behind us. Tell us how you escaped the vest."

Suddenly, the wall behind two of the men exploded. Behdin dropped to the floor as penetrators tore them apart. Blood and gore splattered across him and up the walls. The third man, mortally wounded, fell to the ground screaming as he clutched his entrails.

Behdin scrambled across the floor and dove head first toward the rusty ladder. Missing the rungs he fell through to the floor, landing heavily on his back and knocking the air from his lungs. He lay still for a moment, fighting for breath.

To his horror drops of blood fell from the opening above. Rolling clear he struggled to his feet and staggered through an open hall. More explosions shook the building, and it shuddered and groaned. Chunks of concrete fell from the ceiling as he headed to the opposite side of the dilapidated structure.

The men had told him of the girl in the other group. That had to be Xeyal; she'd been the youngest female in the prison. The others were all men and older women.

Turning a corner Behdin ran into a collapsed ceiling. Slabs of concrete blocked his path. As he contemplated turning back he heard an ominous thudding from behind. Heavy footsteps approached.

Dropping to his knees he crawled under a massive steel beam, wedging himself deep into the rubble. Peering out through a narrow crack he held his breath.

Something appeared in the gloom, shimmering when debris dropped from the ceiling then blending with the grey walls.

Behdin recognized the shape. It was one of the robots. Heart racing he slowly eased his AK into a gap in the rubble and rested his finger on the trigger. Then he remembered what had happened last time he had fired at one of them. Bullets had bounced from its armor and he had ended up unconscious. Attacking was pointless. The only way to survive was to remain hidden until the killer had passed.

He held his breath as the figure paused then stood still. Behdin thought he could hear faint voices over the background noise of the battle outside. The machine, if that's what it was, seemed to be waiting for something.

A massive detonation shook the building and the slab of concrete shifted slightly almost crushing Behdin's arm. He snatched it away, scraping the AK against the rough surface. His heart leaped into his mouth as he glanced back at the robot. In the dust filled air he could see that it was looking directly at him.

It raised an arm and he squeezed the trigger. The bark of the AK was deafening in the confined space. He grit his teeth and held the gun firm as it blasted the robot with bullets. Then, when it ran dry, he discarded it and ducked out from the rubble.

His ears rang as he scrambled past the seemingly dazed robot and sprinted for the end of the corridor. Behind him, he heard a high-pitched whine. The exit was mere feet away when he stumbled on a loose rock and tripped forward, hands outstretched. Before he could regain his balance, he stumbled and crashed to the ground driving his knee into a lump of concrete. He grunted in pain, but immediately struggled to his feet.

Glancing over his shoulder he saw the ghostly machine was only yards away. He franticly glanced left and right, searching for a weapon.

"I know you," a metallic voice said. "You're the one I cut free."

Behdin's hand fell on a short piece of steel and he clenched it as the robot appeared from behind its shimmering cloak. Humanoid in shape it was covered in a matte black finish. He recognized sophisticated weapons on each arm.

Suddenly, its face lifted upward and human features appeared.

"You're a girl," he exclaimed.

The girl's exotic looks and the bulk of the suit made it hard for him to guess her age. He estimated she was at least a couple of years older than him.

She wore a look of concern. "What are you doing here?"

He scowled at her. "I'm trying to find my sister before you and your friends kill her."

Wilda stood for a moment processing what the boy had said. The fact that Sakkin had brought this boy and his sister here to both die sickened and enraged her. She clenched her fists and jaw as fury coursed through her body. When she was done with the *Tsalmaveth* she was going to make the bastards pay. Her gaze fell on the boy's knee, which he was clutching. "Are you injured?"

He shook his head.

"I can help you with that," she said as another explosion shook the building.

"I don't need your help."

She managed a half smile. "You've already had it."

His eyes narrowed. "How?"

"I was the one who took off your vest."

The boy's face changed to a look of confusion. "Why would you do that? You're one of them. You're a killer."

She shook her head. "No. I am like you. I was taken from my family and forced to become something I'm not." She knelt and retrieved a medical kit from her suit.

"They took me and my sister," the boy said as she inspected his knee.

For a split second Wilda was transported back to her village and the violent night when she was taken from her mother. The memory felt like a punch to the chest. She understood the pain this boy must feel.

"Do you know where she is?" Her palm scanner confirmed nothing was broken.

He winced as she held a stimpen against his skin. It let out a hiss, jetting a microscopic dose of anti-inflammatory directly into the joint. "I think so."

As Wilda glanced up at his face she spotted something in the map pocket of his tattered chest rig. "What have you got there?"

He placed his hand over the pouch. "Nothing."

"What's your name?"

"Behdin."

She wrapped a compression bandage around the boy's knee. "And what's your sister's name?"

"Xeyal."

"My name's Wilda, and if you and I are going to find Xeyal, then I'm going to need to have a look at what you've got in there."

The boy's forehead creased as he considered her words. Then, slowly, he slid a cracked flexipad out from behind the AK magazines in his chest rig.

Wilda snatched it from his hands and activated the screen. She managed a wry smile; it was the flexipad she'd lost. Now her position was not so helpless.

"Can you use that to free my sister?"

She nodded as her helmet beeped.

"Eight Two, what's the delay?" The squad leader's transmission was faint due to interference.

Tapping on the flexipad she made sure the concrete walls were blocking her tracking signal and camera feeds.

"Eight Two, answer me."

She sighed before transmitting a reply. "I have eyes on

the target building and I'm evaluating the threat before infiltration. It would be easier if I had drone support."

"Negative, Hunters have not been allocated. We are continuing to draw hostiles away from the objective. You are to move now."

"Yes, sir." She killed the uplink.

Behdin's eyes narrowed. "Who were you talking to?"

"The people who took your sister. They don't know I'm working against them."

The boy nodded. "If they knew, they would kill you, like they kill everyone else."

Wilda met the boy's serious gaze. Staring into his eyes, she recognized the distant look that came with exposure to violence. She fought the urge to hug him and instead secured her medical kit and checked her flexipad. "Your sister should be in the target with the others. You wait here and I'll make entry and locate her."

He shook his head. "No. I'm coming with you."

"It's too dangerous."

"She's my sister. I'm not staying behind." He stood and tested his knee. Then he moved back to the pile of rubble and recovered his AK.

Wilda followed, dropping her faceplate before deactivating her suit's camera feed. She caught up with Behdin as he made to exit the corridor. "Things are going to get pretty hectic." She moved past him. "The safest place to be is behind me."

Xeyal hugged her knees as gunfire and explosions echoed through the concrete building where the robots had left her. Eyes wide with terror she watched as men and women dashed back and forth carrying weapons. One of the men had already taken her AK and ammunition. It was best, she didn't think she could use it.

She had searched the entire building for Behdin when she first arrived, but found no trace. No one had seen her brother or any of the other men who had left the prison with him.

Attempting to leave the building was suicide. Two men had tried to flee. Their vests had detonated, killing them instantly.

"You poor thing." The voice was soft despite the chaos of the battle.

She looked up into a friendly face shrouded in a black hijab.

"Is there anyone with you?" the woman asked as she squatted beside her.

She shook her head.

"How old are you?"

"I'm twelve."

The woman sighed. "That's too young. These people are dogs." Reaching out she gently stroked Xeyal's hair. "My daughter is four." She smiled grimly. "I will never see her again, but at least she is with my family."

A loud beep emitted from the woman's vest.

"I must go." She placed her hand gently on Xeyal's cheek. "May Allah be with you."

She departed, leaving Xeyal with a feeling of utter isolation. Glancing in the direction the woman had gone she contemplated following. A series of loud explosions dispelled the thought and she curled back into a ball.

An even larger blast rocked the entire building and Xeyal let out a whimper. Pieces of the ceiling dropped around her as men yelled and weapons barked.

A strange crackling noise filled the air. It reminded her of the time lightning had struck close to her father's flock. She felt the hairs on her arm stand on end as the noise sounded again.

Two armed men appeared from her right. A ball of energy struck each of them and they collapsed to the ground.

She let out a piercing scream and huddled in the corner.

"Xeyal, is that you?"

Instantly recognizing Behdin's voice she clambered to her feet and ran toward it. She had only taken a few steps when she froze in horror. A tall shimmering figure stood between her and her brother.

"It's OK, Xeyal. She's here to help." Behdin stepped past the figure and wrapped his arms around her.

Tears spilled from her eyes as she hugged him. "I thought you were…"

"Well, I'm not." He pried himself from her grip and placed both arms on her shoulders. "We need to get this vest off. Then we can go home."

Behind him the shimmering figure turned into a black robot. It reached two hands to its head. A moment later, the face of a girl, not much older than her brother, appeared. It was then she realized that it was not a robot at all. It was a person inside a suit. "Are they all people?" she asked as girl examined a tablet.

"No, some of them are robots."

"It's dead. You can take it off," the girl in the suit said.

Xeyal continued to stare at the suited girl as her brother drew a knife and cut the vest at her shoulders. Then he tossed it on the floor.

"Now, get her out of here," the girl snapped before her mask dropped back in place.

"Who is she?" Xeyal asked as Behdin unslung an assault rifle and led her away.

They paused at the entrance to a stairwell and he glanced back. "She's a friend."

Shadow Runner, Syria

Leon Wilkin slammed his fist down on the operations table and the two operations officers jumped. "What the fuck is going on? Why can't I see where trainee Eight Two is? Why can't I see the feeds from her damn cameras?"

"Sir, she may be underground."

He scowled at the man. "How the hell would she maneuver a half-ton exoskeleton underground?"

"They're equipped with the jumper suits," the officer replied.

He leaned across the table and stared at him. "She's not underground. She's in the city and somehow she's figured out how to jam the suit's signal."

Slumping into a chair, he turned and spotted a smug look on Marnisha's elfin features. "You think this is funny? Your little project has gone rogue. You've failed."

She shrugged. "Eight Two is displaying resourcefulness and adaptability. That pleases me greatly."

"I'm sure it fucking does."

"Sir, one of the OFTs just went offline at the target building," reported an officer.

"KIA or a glitch?"

The man's fingers danced on the glass surface. "Neither, a twelve year old girl has disappeared. Her vest is no longer in the network."

"This fits Eight Two's profile," said Shona. "If she can shield her own signature perhaps she worked out a way to free the OFT's. She is overly compassionate."

"That's unlikely," said the officer.

Leon turned to Marnisha, who was glaring at Shona. "Is she capable of that?"

She shrugged. "You're the one who trained her."

"If she's hacked the system it's terms for termination," said Shona.

Eight Two's icon flashed on the operations table, inside the target building. Leon reached out and stabbed it with his finger. "Eight Two, report your status."

A hiss of static sounded from the speakers above the table. "This is Eight Two, was engaged by heavy weapons. Have sustained superficial damage. HUD and comms are intermittent, moving now to terminate objective."

"Run a diagnostic on her suit," he ordered.

The officer activated the required commands. "I'm unable to access her suit. Her communications module is most likely damaged."

Leon pondered the information. "Bring Seven Nine Nine in closer. I want him to confirm target neutralization."

"Will do."

"Run the status of all the OFTs. I want to know if any of them have been tampered with."

It took a moment for the officer to run the request. "Fifteen OFTs are KIA. Eight are unconscious; all of those are in the target compound."

He shook his head. "She can't even kill." He slapped his hand on the table. "The training standards are clear. If she fails the *Tsalmaveth*, she will be terminated."

"Calm down, Leon," snapped Marnisha. "She will complete her mission, give her time."

He glared at the scientist before switching to Shona, sitting alongside. The psychologist's plump lip curled at the corner. He fought the urge to do the same. Doctor Marnisha Copeland would be severely disappointed when her little project failed.

"Deploy drones. I want to see what that bitch is up to."

Homs, Syria

Wilda spun around as a cluster of lead pellets struck her armor. Raising her arm she returned fire with her pulsar emitter.

The shotgun-wielding assailant collapsed to the floor, knocked unconscious by a burst of static energy. She contemplated deactivating his vest but didn't have time, her squad would be close behind. A glance at her HUD told her she was almost on top of her objective. It was behind the rusted steel door that the now unconscious man had been guarding.

She knew there would be an innocent prisoner on the other side; a target that Sakkin needed to believe she had neutralized. Her thermal sensor had confirmed it, what looked like a man sitting on a chair.

Through her helmet's speakers she heard the distinctive whir of a hunter drone. She spotted it through the ruined frontage of the building. It hovered, watching her.

Moving swiftly she put a wall between her and the drone. Then she ripped a charge from a pouch and slapped it on the wall. Standing alongside, she detonated it.

The smart charge shattered the concrete wall. She stepped through the breach into a confined space clouded with dust and smoke. She could see the outline of her target through her HUD; a figure strapped to a chair. She grit her teeth. Her Sakkin masters wanted her to slaughter a tethered goat.

As the dust settled and the smoke cleared the situation became even more sinister. The man they expected her to murder was Henry.

Her friend moaned, battered and bruised with his head slumped forward and chin resting on a Sakkin prisoner vest.

"Henry!" she rushed to him.

He managed to lift his head. "Wilda, is that you?"

Using the flexipad she deactivated his vest, then drew her knife and cut his bonds. Tears streamed from her eyes as she freed her friend.

"You have to kill me," he said hoarsely. "If you don't they'll terminate you."

She removed the vest before using her scanner to check his health. "No. I'm going to save you." His wounds were superficial.

He reached up and grasped her suit, his eyes misty. "You need to protect yourself. Kill me and you will graduate. Then you can bring Sakkin down from the inside."

Wilda shook her head and scooped him up like a child. "No. We're both getting out of here. We'll take our chances with Sakkin, together."

Chapter Thirteen

Shadow Runner, Syria

Thirty thousand feet above the city of Homs Leon, Marnisha and Shona watched the feed from one of the drones.

"Sir, Eight Two's target is offline," reported an operations officer.

"She's set him free," snapped Leon.

On screen he saw a figure appear from the building's strong room. The drone's camera focused on a shimmering figure carrying the crippled weapons technician. He turned to Marnisha. "The evidence is conclusive. I'm ordering Eight Two's termination."

Her eyes narrowed. "You're not authorized–"

"Yes, I am. She's failed the *Tsalmaveth*. That's a death sentence." He nodded at the operations officer. "Terminate her."

"Yes, sir."

He turned his attention back to the drone feed. There

was a flash as Eight Two fired her railer directly at them. The screen went blank.

"Sir, I'm unable to execute the command. She's disappeared from the network. Termination sequence has failed."

Leon clenched his jaw. "Link me with Seven Nine Nine."

"Online."

"Seven Nine Nine, you are to eliminate Eight Two along with any OFTs in her vicinity. She is not to escape."

A hiss of static marked the squad leader's reply. "It will be done."

"We will launch additional hunter drones to augment your efforts." He shot Marnisha a smirk. "I guess we're going to see how capable your little toy is."

She shrugged. "It looks like she's already one step ahead of you."

"How many OPFOR mechops are still operational?"

"Six," replied the operations officer.

"Assign them to Seven Nine Nine. Let's see how Eight Two handles an army."

Homs, Syria

Seven Nine Nine barely suppressed the glee in his voice as he ordered the newly allocated mechops to surround the building where Eight Two was last seen.

This was his opportunity to show the head trainer what he was capable of. The fact the mission was to destroy Eight Two was the icing on the cake.

His battle map showed him when the clankers were in position. He had updated their kill orders to include everyone other than his team. They would slaughter anyone who tried to exit the building.

"Tree, you're with me," he transmitted. "The rest of you are in reserve."

The members of squad *Gurion* remained silent as he ran a system check and confirmed his jumper suit as fully functional. Glancing sideways he saw Tree doing the same. He opened a private channel to the tall teen.

"We're not going to have any problems, are we?"

"No, why would we?"

"Because you respect Eight Two."

"Why would that impact the mission? We've been ordered to terminate her and that's exactly what we will do."

Seven Nine Nine extended the black carbon blade attached to his railer. It snapped into place and he raised it in the air. "Good! The kill is mine. You're backup. Stay out of the way and you'll learn a thing or two."

Wilda's mind raced as she carried Henry up a flight of stairs toward the rooftop. She knew Seven Nine Nine would come from the bottom, expecting to trap her on the roof or at least expose her to the hunter drones.

"You should leave me and go," croaked Henry when they reached the sun-scorched roof.

She placed him in the shade of a rusted air-conditioning unit. "No, I'm going to get us both out of here."

"Give me the flexipad."

Leaving him with the device she dashed across the roof to the side. The building opposite was less than thirty yards away.

Crouching she ejected the equipment pack from the back of her suit. Inside she found a soft pouch containing a steel dart linked to a coil of thin polymer rope and a power pulley. As she loaded the dart into the end of her railer her augmented hearing detected the buzz of a drone.

The disc-shaped craft appeared over the lip of the building. Ignoring it she aimed at the building opposite and fired the dart.

It shot across the gap, trailing the cable and slammed into the distant rooftop. Another drone joined the first as she tied the cable to a steel railing and pulled it tight. She hooked the power pulley onto the taut line and activated the brake.

"Henry, we're leaving!" she yelled as she ran back to where she had left him in the shade. She was halfway when a shimmering figure exploded from the rooftop door, blocking her way.

The figure fired as she dove for cover. She felt a round penetrate the side of her armor, narrowly missing her torso. Another hissed past and something struck her weapon. Alarms flashed in her helmet and her railer went offline.

Hunkering in behind a ventilation shaft she slung the damaged railer across her back.

"Make this easy on everyone and surrender," an amplified voice called out. It was Seven Nine Nine. "You're alone now. No one is going to help you."

A feeling of utter helplessness washed over Wilda. He was right. She exhaled. "If I surrender will you make sure nothing happens to Henry?"

"Who the hell is Henry?"

"The technician." She unclipped a ball scanner from her rig and rolled it out from behind cover. The device transmitted its feed directly into her HUD.

Seven Nine Nine stood in the open with a railer aimed in her direction. There was no sign of Henry or anyone else. She yanked a plasma grenade from her belt. As she armed the grenade she heard a loud buzzing from above.

She glanced up and saw that five of the hunter drones hovered together. Usually they flew alone or sometimes in pairs.

As she watched, the hunters moved into a strange formation. Two went high with two others lower and closer together. The fifth had positioned itself central between the two groups. It was almost as if they were forming the letter W.

One of the drones dove as she rolled out of cover and tossed the grenade. The nimble craft slammed into Seven Nine Nine's helmet, knocking him backward as he fired. Hypervelocity penetrators snapped over her head as the grenade detonated, engulfing the squad leader in molten plasma.

Henry appeared on the opposite side of the doorway. He held the flexipad in one hand as he dragged himself with the other. Wilda dashed to his side and lifted him from the ground.

"I'll be damned if we're not going down without a fight," he barked as he clung to her suit.

She ran to where she had left the pulley. Grasping it with her gauntlet she took a running leap off the building.

More penetrators hissed past as the clankers below opened fire, but then they were clear of the gap. Landing heavily she spun and saw a figure standing at their point of departure. From the size she knew it had to be Tree. She braced, anticipating a volley of railer rounds.

They never eventuated. She dashed across the roof with Henry, dropping over a ledge onto another building.

"We need to get underground," said Henry. "The only safe place is beneath the city."

"Only if we can get past the clankers and the rest of squad *Gurion*."

"All you have to do is outthink them Wilda. That's your strength and it's something they can't defend against."

She dropped through a blast hole into what was once a laboratory. No pressure, she thought as they made their way through the building. We only have to evade a dozen clankers and a team of assassins, all the while armed only with a knife.

Seven Nine Nine felt like he was floating on a cloud, a soft warm cloud that enveloped his entire body. Then with a flash it was gone and he was back in his suit staring up at the dusty brown sky.

"You have suffered significant burns to your torso," announced his suit in a soft feminine voice. "I have applied a nerve block and administered enhancers."

"Report on suit," he said.

"Systems are coming back online. All weapons are operable. However, your core armor has been degraded. Recommend immediate evacuation for technical and medical support."

He clambered to his feet. "Recommendation noted. Maintain weapon systems as a priority. Terminate non-essential functions as required."

He glanced around. Pieces of shattered drone littered the rooftop and a patch of concrete was charred black. Fortunately his suit and a now destroyed air conditioner had absorbed most of the blast from Eight Two's grenade.

"Where is Tree?" he queried.

"I'm here."

He turned to face him.

"They fled to the west. Additional drones have been deployed and have isolated them to a single compound," the teen reported. "I've ordered clankers and the rest of the team to surround it. I figured you would want to go in yourself."

"How long was I out?"

"A matter of minutes. They haven't gotten far."

"Good." He checked the charge on his railer. "She's out of tricks. This time I'm going to cut off her head."

Shadow Runner, Syria

Leon frowned as he watched a replay of Eight Two's escape from Seven Nine Nine. He had never seen anything like it. Somehow, she had managed to override the orders to the drones and use them as a weapon. He turned to Marnisha, who was also studying the feed. "How did she do that?"

Her lip curled. "How would I know? You're the one responsible for her training."

"Yes and it didn't include how to hack our systems."

One of the operations officers spoke up, "Sir, there's an admin flexipad on the network in the same vicinity as Eight Two."

Leon's eyes narrowed. "Shut it down."

"The technician must have taught her how to use it," said Shona.

"What technician?" asked Marnisha.

Shona shot Leon a sheepish look. He nodded,

prompting her to answer. "The target she was supposed to terminate is a technician she befriended."

Marnisha's eyes narrowed. "The two of you are psychopaths. I'm trying to develop an empathetic operative capable of operating clandestinely amongst indigenous populations and you decide to have her assassinate her first contact?"

"She has no loyalty to Sakkin," said Shona.

"No, not now she doesn't. Your sheer idiocy has turned her against us."

"That doesn't ma—"

Marnisha raised her hand. "If you speak again I'll have you transferred to a mine in Antarctica."

"She's right. It doesn't matter," snapped Leon. "Eight Two has betrayed Sakkin and failed the *Tsalmaveth*. There is nothing more to discuss."

Marnisha shot him an icy glare.

"Sir, do you want me to deploy additional mechops?" interrupted one of the operations officers.

"No. Seven Nine Nine has all the assets he needs. Confirm his status?"

"He has severe burns, but there is no immediate risk to his life. His jumper suit has an estimated two hours of power remaining. Do you want me to coordinate his extraction for treatment?"

Leon shook his head. "No. I want Eight Two terminated within the hour."

Marnisha rose from the table. "Good luck with that." She directed her attention to the operations officer. "Have my vertjet prepared."

"Leaving early?" Leon asked.

She stared at him. "I've seen more than enough."

"Enough to know your little project has failed?"

The corners of her mouth turned up giving the faintest hint of a smile. "Just deviations from the plan." She turned and strode from the bridge, her heels ringing against the deck.

"What did she mean by that?" asked Shona when she was gone.

He shrugged. "Who cares?" Turning he fixed his attention on one of the monitors on the wall. Blue icons were forming a ring around a cluster of buildings. "Eight Two will be dead before Marnisha's engines are warm."

Chapter Fourteen

Homs, Syria

Wilda deactivated her jumper suit, raised the faceplate leaving the helmet attached, and stepped out of it. Powered down, its carbon nanotube muscles went rigid and she left the damaged suit standing. She detached her knife from the suit, retrieved a compact radio from a pouch and laid them on the floor alongside the, now inactive, flexipad.

"What are you doing?" asked Henry from where he sat propped against a concrete wall.

She had carried him through the remains of a science facility into the basement. There among empty gas cylinders and rusted equipment she had paused to take stock of their situation.

"If I have to carry you I can't protect us." She struggled to help him from the ground. "The suit will give you mobility."

"Wilda, I haven't walked in decades."

She helped him inside the synthetic armor; she had

adjusted the settings to accommodate his larger frame. The suit barely fit over his broad shoulders and arms. "I've set the suit to run via neural inputs. You only have to think to move."

The suit closed around him, leaving only his face visible underneath the raised faceplate. "I, I don't, I don't know how."

"Henry, if you can't walk then we're both going to die here." She attached her knife and radio to the lightweight underarmor vest that was now her only protection.

Henry's brow furrowed as he focused on moving the suit. For a full minute he willed the quarter ton of titanium, carbon, electronics and artificial muscle to move.

"I don't think I can do it."

Wilda touched his cheek. "Yes, you can. Clear your mind and remember a time when you could run. Remember playing with your daughter, running on a beach with her."

Tears formed in the corners of his eyes and ran along the creases in his weathered face. He let out a deep breath and closed them.

She watched with trepidation as the suit shuddered. Slowly, the right foot lifted and slid forward a few inches.

"Henry, you're doing it," she whispered.

His eyes opened and he broke into a smile. "I remember." He took tentative steps, clomping around the basement. "It's like riding a damn bike," he muttered, raising the suit's arms into the air.

As Henry practiced, Wilda searched for an exit. She checked every wall, to no avail. The only way in or out was through the ground level, above them. In one corner she found a pile of rags. Rifling through it she found a robe and wrapped it around her shoulders.

"Henry, we need to get moving. We need to go back up. Are you ready?"

He stomped awkwardly across the room. "Yes, I can do it."

"OK, let's go. I'll scout ahead." She took the compact radio from her belt. "You move when I give you the all clear." She climbed a staircase into a corridor. Clutching her knife she crouched low and made her way toward the outer rooms.

Through a blast hole in a wall she spotted a dark figure moving. She ducked back as it passed.

A moment later she edged forward to where she could see outside. Light was fading fast. She identified a clanker next to a distant building, its weapon aimed toward them. Another stood behind the blackened remains of a tank.

They would be the outer cordon, the blocking force. It told her that the assault team would come from another side. As she turned she heard boots crunch in the rubble. She gripped her knife. In the failing light she spotted Henry's sheepish features beneath the raised faceplate of the jumper suit.

She lowered the blade. "I told you to stay put."

"We should stick together."

As he stepped closer she could see his eyes were clear and alert. The suit's internal medical sensors had detected and treated his injuries. Wilda, on the other hand, felt fatigued in the stifling heat, the downside to training in climate-controlled suits. "OK, but you have to do what I say."

He raised a gauntlet in a salute. "Yes, ma'am."

As she waved him forward Wilda heard another sound from deeper within the building. It was a noise she knew all too well; the whine and clank of mechops on the move.

Her chest tightened as she searched frantically for a way out.

Right as she considered a mad dash past the clankers she spotted a small figure beyond them. Without the vision enhancement offered by her helmet she almost missed the boy crouched in the rubble.

Despite the gloom she recognized the teen that she had rescued, Behdin. As she stared he gestured with an extended thumb, indicating for her to go to his left.

"Friend of yours?" asked Henry.

She glanced over her shoulder at the suited technician.

"You could say that."

"You trust him?"

"That doesn't matter. At this point in time, he's our only way out." She heard the whine of a railer powering up. "Move!"

Seven Nine Nine stepped through a blast hole in the wall of the building where Eight Two had been sighted. He could see clearly through the gloom; his vision augmented by thermal and multispectral sensors.

A red icon appeared on his HUD as a drone spotted movement on the far side of the bullet-riddled structure. He aimed for the mark and fired his railer, shattering the concrete wall.

Suddenly an explosion detonated from his right flank. The HUD automatically switched to a drone feed and he watched as a ball of orange flame rolled up into the sky. "What was that?"

"Two of the clankers are checking it out," replied one of the trainees from the outer cordon.

"No, it's a diversion. Keep them focused on this building," he transmitted.

There was a pause before an alert chimed and a drone spun away from the blast. Through its camera he caught a glimpse of two shapes darting across the open ground between the building he was in and another.

"You idiots, you've let them escape." He broke into a run, smashing through an internal wall like it was cardboard. Exiting onto the street he oriented himself, identifying the spot where Eight Two had disappeared. "Mechops on me," he ordered. Immediately the two closest clankers joined him, one on each side.

"Do you want us to pursue?" asked Tree.

"No, the bitch is mine." He charged between two small apartment blocks into a rubble-strewn courtyard.

He spotted three figures a hundred yards distant, one in a jumper suit. They were weaving between burnt cars and craters, heading toward a multi-story complex beyond a square.

His HUD locked onto them with hostile markers. He raised his railer and fired. Either side of him the mechops followed his lead adding the blast of their own weapons to the maelstrom.

The suit's sensors lost track of the targets and he ordered the clankers to cease-fire.

"Cover me," he ordered as he stalked forward for the kill.

"Henry!" Wilda screamed as the technician staggered, the jumper suit sparking as a penetrator tore through the armor.

He toppled sideways as more shots cut through the air where he previously stood.

Crawling over rocks and debris she reached his side. "Henry, are you alive?" There was no reply as she checked the display on the suit's arm. A sequence of flashing icons told her that he was stable but critical. The suit had administered a coagulant into the wound and was maintaining his oxygen and circulation.

Hearing a rustle from behind she spun. The boy, Behdin, crouched a few feet away with his AK clutched in his hands. "Your friend, is he dead?"

"No, the suit's keeping him alive. I need to do the same for us." She reached for the AK.

He stared at her for a moment before shuffling across and passing it to her. She checked the ancient weapon as she slid behind a low wall that bounded a raised garden bed.

She spotted Seven Nine Nine fifty yards away. He moved steadily toward them, the blade attached to his railer extended. Slightly behind him a pair of jetblack clankers moved off to each flank, barely visible in the failing light.

Her plan was to draw them away from Henry, then double back, and find a way to get him to safety. She knew the odds of that happening were next to none. Armed with an AK and up against clankers and ganics, she was as good as dead.

She raised the weapon. As she squeezed the trigger she faintly registered a flash.

As the rifle bucked in her shoulder the entire world seemed to burst into flame. Rockets screamed from the buildings on either side and slammed into the ground around Seven Nine Nine and his clankers. She watched in awe as the earth erupted like a volcano. A blast of intense heat lifted her from the ground and blew her back against the building behind her. Her breath was driven from her lungs as she hit the wall, her head snapping backward. Darkness flooded her brain as she slumped to the ground.

Shadow Runner, Syria

Leon watched from behind thick glass as the aerostat's hangar doors closed beneath the arriving MX22. A green light flashed when the hold had been pressurized then the vertjet's rear ramp snapped open.

"Take him directly to the infirmary," he ordered as two medical mechops descended from the vertjet carrying a casualty on a stretcher. The order was redundant, but Leon needed an outlet for the rage building inside him.

Despite having the deck stacked against her, Eight Two had run rings around him, his staff and his trainees. Somehow, she had managed to ambush Seven Nine Nine, critically wound him and destroy two mechops before disappearing.

The rack of hunter drones on the opposite side of the hangar was almost empty. There were ten of them still scouring the city for Eight Two. Squad *Gurion* was also on the ground with another six mechops. His eyes narrowed as he considered sending the rest of his forces to assist in the search. No, he would rely on the training resources before deploying his reserve.

Leaving the hangar he strode along one of the narrow corridors that ran the length of the *Shadow Runner*. When he reached the infirmary he slid the door back and stepped inside.

The medical mechops had loaded Seven Nine Nine, still in his jumper suit, into a medical pod.

He moved across and peered in at the wounded trainee.

It was not Leon's first rodeo when it came to battlefield casualties. He had seen his fair share, but he had never seen a body so badly burned yet still alive.

The squad leader's jumper suit was mangled and scorched. How it had managed to keep him alive was nothing short of amazing. Through rents in the armor he could see molten flesh and charred muscle. Half of his jaw was missing with the face above it burnt almost to the skull. His right eye socket was completely empty, the eyeball having popped from the heat.

As he watched, the pod's half-dozen mechanical arms cut and lifted the jumper suit away from the horrifically injured body. In seconds they had inserted IV lines, replacing the life support provided by the suit.

"Is he going to be all right?" asked Shona from behind him.

He had not heard her enter over the hum of the medical pod. "He's not going to die, but I'll doubt he'll be much use to Sakkin now."

"They could rebuild him."

"Not worth the expense." He turned and left the infirmary, returning to the bridge.

"Have they found her?" he asked, leaning over the operations table.

"No, sir. Three Three, the new squad leader, has requested additional assets to assist in the search," replied one of his staff.

"He'll do as he's told. The *Tsalmaveth* is over. I want every training asset out hunting or patrolling the training area. Be forewarned, she is going to make a break for the desert. When she does, we'll be ready."

"Shall I commit the gen-seven mechops?"

Leon shook his head. "No! We have sufficient assets to deal with this. Hold them in reserve."

He left the table and moved to the observation deck where he could gaze at the city of Homs, thirty thousand feet below. From this height it was a brown smudge on a sea of yellow sand. Beyond it the sun was low on the horizon. Soon the city would be dark, giving his forces the advantage.

He folded his hands in the small of his back as he studied the city. "Where are you hiding, Eight Two? Come out from under your rock so I can crush you."

Homs, Syria

Wilda's eyes opened and she clutched at her forearm, searching franticly for her knife. As she realized it was missing, a voice spoke, "We removed it."

She turned her head and found herself on a bunk in a dingy concrete-walled room. The voice belonged to a man with a patchy beard and bulbous nose. He wore jeans, boots and a T-shirt that had once been black but had faded to gray. An AK-47 lay across his knees as he sat on a wooden box, smoking.

"I'm sorry. It is merely a security precaution. Once we know you a little better you can have it back."

Wilda touched the back of her head as she sat up on the edge of the bunk. She winced as her fingers found a tender lump.

"Are they all as young as you?" asked the man.

She nodded.

He wore a bleak expression. "What has this world come to?" Then he stubbed out his cigarette. "My name is Hanan and you are now a guest of the underground." He rose from the box. "Come, your friends are waiting for you."

Wilda stood then the room suddenly blurred. She reached out for a wall and steadied herself. As the fog lifted from her brain she remembered the last moments of the battle. "Henry, where is Henry?"

"Your friend in the suit? We've hidden him. The boy, Behdin, insisted that we not try to remove him from it. He said it was keeping him alive."

"He's right. You need to take me to him now."

Hanan nodded as he gestured to a doorway draped with a blanket. "Yes of course, but first you must meet the others."

Wilda ambled to the opening and pushed the material away, revealing a much larger room. Electric lamps hung from a high arched ceiling. In the center was a long table where Behdin and his sister sat side-by-side eating from matching plastic bowls.

She glanced around. Among the shelves and boxes of military hardware other men stared at her. They were dressed similarly to Hanan, a rag-tag crew armed with battered assault rifles and haggard expressions.

"Who are you people?" she asked.

A gray-bearded man wearing a battered pair of spectacles stepped forward. "The real question is, who are you?"

For a moment, she had no response. No one had ever asked that question before. It took her a moment to realize that she was no longer Eight Two the Sakkin trainee. She was finally free from her number and her former masters.

"My name is Wilda. I was a Sakkin trainee. Now I am free and I need to help my friend Henry before he dies."

"She could be a spy," one of the other men stated.

"She's not a spy," declared Behdin from the table. "She saved my sister and me."

"That doesn't stop her from being a Sakkin spy," snapped the man.

"Why would I spy for Sakkin?" said Wilda. "They took me from my mother and probably killed her. They enslave innocent people and force orphaned teenagers to massacre them. They take children and turn them into mindless killers. I despise Sakkin and I'm going to destroy them."

The man with the glasses stepped closer and examined her face. She held his gaze, their eyes locked. "She's telling the truth."

"I don't have time for this." She looked around. "My friend is dying."

"Of course," he said, turning to Hanan. "Her friend is the key to our success."

Wilda frowned. "What do you mean by that?"

"We have a weapon that will allow us to free the prisoners who are still alive and leave this place."

"What kind of weapon?"

The man turned to Hanan, who nodded. Then he returned to Wilda. "A weapon that will destroy Sakkin's circuits. The Americans once called it CHAMP."

Wilda glanced around the room again, taking in the outdated weaponry and rudimentary conditions. She found it difficult to believe that these men could possess such a device.

"It's true," said Hanan. "Eon was a scientist with Sakkin. He built the missile from parts. The only thing missing is the power source."

Her eyes narrowed. "You need the ultracapacitor from my suit? The only thing keeping Henry alive?"

Hanan nodded.

"You want me to sacrifice my friend for a homemade weapon that might not work?"

"The weapon will work," declared Eon.

She shook her head. "You will need Henry to look at it."

"Why, what does he know about such things?"

"He's a Sakkin weapons technician."

The man's eyes lit up.

"Now, take me to him."

Hanan waved his team into one corner of the room, leaving Wilda at the table with Behdin and his sister.

"They're scared," said the boy.

"We all are, but together we can escape."

He nodded. "I need to get my sister home. Our mother will be worried."

Wilda's eyes misted as she watched the two children eating together. Family was a relatively new concept to her and something she had not had time to reflect on in the last few days. In fact, the only real family she had was Henry and right now, he was alone and injured. She turned to the men of the underground. "If you're not going to help me I'll go by myself."

The men broke from their huddle and Hanan strode toward her. "I will take you."

Behdin rose from the bench and grabbed his AK from where it leaned against the wall. "I will come too."

"You should stay with your sister," said Wilda.

He shook his head. "You saved our lives. We have a debt to you."

She shrugged. "OK, then. Take me to Henry."

Hanan reached into his pocket and handed over her

knife. Then he took an AK and a bandolier of magazines from atop an ammunition crate and thrust them into her arms. "Every robot and every drone is searching for you. We need to be cautious."

Wilda loaded and cocked the rifle. "With tools like these, we better stay out of sight. We won't stand a chance against a clanker or a ganic."

Hanan picked up a rifle and a backpack as he made for the door. "That is why we will remain below the surface. It's the only place we are safe."

Chapter Fifteen

Shadow Runner, Syria

Leon drummed his fingers on the digital map as he watched icons denoting hunter drones and mechops progressing through Homs' ruined streets. He had over thirty assets committed to the hunt and so far not one of them had found even the slightest trace of Eight Two or the people who had assisted her.

"Sir."

His eyes snapped to the officer who had spoken.

"Seven Nine Nine is requesting a new jumper suit and reinsertion into the Area of Operations."

"What is his status?"

"The medical facility has cleared him for sedentary duties."

"Have him report here." Leon returned his attention back to the digital map. A green zone showed the area that had already been searched; it covered all of the university and was rapidly expanding outward.

Engrossed in his analysis Leon did not hear the door to the bridge open.

"Sir, I know where they are."

The croaking voice startled him and he glanced up at a hideously disfigured face. One-half of Seven Nine Nine's features looked as if they had been melted by a blowtorch. His right eyeball was missing, the socket filled with synthetic flesh. Sakkin had the technology to give the man back his sight but Leon knew they would never authorize the expenditure; Seven Nine Nine was no longer a high-value asset.

Leon stared into the teenager's remaining eye as he rose. "Where are they?"

"Will you let me go after them?"

"What did you say?" snarled Leon as he dropped his hand to his pistol. "Insubordination warrants immediate termination."

There was no fear in what remained of Seven Nine Nine's face. His single eye burned with hatred, the veins in his ruined flesh pulsed. "They're underground. That's the only way they could avoid the hunter drones."

Leon took his hand from the pistol and rested it on the battle map as he considered the assessment. "Display subterranean data."

"Yes, sir," replied one of the operations officers.

A moment later a new layer appeared on the map. A network of tunnels, pipes and cables spiderwebbed across the city.

"Of course," whispered Leon.

"Not all of them will be big enough to allow human movement," said Seven Nine Nine. "If you remove the smaller ones, the network will be easier to search."

The officer followed the recommendation and the network thinned.

"Good work," said Leon.

Seven Nine Nine turned to him with an earnest look in his eye. "Can I join the others—"

"No," Leon said cutting him off. "You'll work here and assist my staff in coordinating the search."

"But—"

"Be thankful you're still alive." Leon turned his attention back to the battle map. "Have the mechops gain access to one of the larger tunnels and see if we can get hunter drones inside. Then check our weapons inventory for flamers and plasma grenades." He smirked. "Sometimes the best way to hunt is to flush your prey from the brush, with fire."

Homs, Syria

Wilda followed Hanan along a storm drain broad enough to fit a compact car. The underground leader carried a luminescent glow rod and in the faint light it cast on the walls she could see that the tunnels were in poor condition. Sections had deteriorated exposing rusted steel.

"How much further?" she whispered when they paused at a junction.

"It's up ahead," replied Hanan as Behdin joined them. "Part of the tunnel has collapsed giving us access up to a basement. Your friend is hidden inside."

"Let's go then."

As they stepped off Wilda sensed a faint vibration in the walls. It grew in intensity as they progressed. Soon the ceiling and floor were shaking as something heavy passed overhead.

"Look out!" yelled Hanan.

She stepped sideways as a massive chunk of concrete fell and slammed into the ground.

"Stay close to the walls," said Hanan over the racket. Dust and cement dropped around them until the rumbling receded.

"What was that?" asked Behdin.

"One of their robots," said Hanan as he led them along the pipe. "Let's hope there hasn't been a cave in."

"We should hurry," said Wilda.

A few hundred feet further along Hanan stopped in front of a damaged section of the tunnel. Squatting he used the light to inspect the waist-high opening.

He shook his head, confirming Wilda's fears. "The tunnel has collapsed. We need to clear it. Your friend is on the other side."

Working in a chain it took them a little over fifteen minutes to move enough rubble to the point where Wilda could squeeze through. Hanan had tried to stop her, but she grabbed his glow rod and shimmied through.

A short distance along the tunnel she clambered over chunks of concrete leading up into a basement. She held out the light and spotted the outline of a prostrate jumper suit.

A quick inspection of the suit's system panel confirmed that Henry was alive and stable. The suit had induced a coma after its attempts to call a MEDEVAC had failed.

"Is he alive?" Behdin asked, having followed her.

"Yes, for now." She checked the torso and found the damage on the right-hand side. The pencil-thin penetrator had punched clean through. She confirmed that the hole had self-sealed, but knew the internal damage would be significant.

She then used the touchpad on the suit's arm to run a diagnostic. The energy source was intact and the suit functioning. However, Henry's status was critical. Without a medical pod, he would soon die.

As Wilda's chest tightened with grief she heard a scraping sound above. It sounded like someone was digging.

There was no time for tears. She used the touchpad to access the life support system.

"We need to go," hissed Hanan as he recovered his light.

Debris and dust fell as she found the menu she wanted. Her finger hovered over the icon that would induce a cocktail of chemicals to revive Henry from his coma. She wavered; waking him would almost certainly condemn him to death in a matter of hours.

"He's a soldier," Behdin said softly. "He deserves one last chance to fight."

She turned to face the boy. In the gloom she could see the compassion in his eyes. He was right. Heavy banging from above her spurred her into action and she stabbed the icon with her finger.

The result was almost instantaneous. The suit jolted and Henry's hands reached for the railer wound.

"Henry, it's OK."

He sat up and turned his helmeted face toward her. "What the hell happened?" he croaked.

More dust fell from the ceiling and Wilda registered the whine of a servomotor. "There's no time to explain. We need to get out of here."

Henry groaned as he climbed to his feet and staggered after her. Ahead, Behdin dove through the gap as the sound above grew in intensity.

"Is this the only way out?" Henry asked, struggling to maneuver the jumper suit in the confined space.

"You'll need to smash your way out." Behind them, a section of wall collapsed. "I'll cover you."

"No, you go." Henry pushed her toward the hole.

Scrambling through she heard him attacking the rock, enlarging the opening. Emerging she came face to face with a concerned Hanan.

"Is he coming?" the underground leader said, shining his glow rod into the gap.

"Yes, but so is Sakkin. They're digging their way in."

"Then we need to go."

Slabs of concrete toppled into the tunnel and the black-suited figure of Henry appeared. As he stepped through the cavity a sharp crack sounded from behind him and a tungsten penetrator smashed through the brickwork.

"Go, they're right behind me!" he yelled.

Wilda took off along the tunnel after Behdin and Hanan, glancing over her shoulder to check that Henry was keeping up. Despite his wound he was right behind her.

As they skidded around a corner a volley of penetrators narrowly missed Henry, slamming into the wall behind him.

Wilda saw Hanan stop ahead. He yanked a handle from his backpack and slung it onto the ground. She smelled the acrid scent of a burning fuse.

"Go, go, go!" he bellowed, waving them past.

Behind them heavy footfalls echoed.

Wilda sprinted as fast as her legs would carry her, closing the gap with Behdin. Grabbing his hand, she dragged him around another corner.

Her boots slapped through stagnant water as they reached an open chamber. Hanan appeared with Henry hot on his heels.

Hanan waved his glow rod toward to an opening a few yards distant. "In there."

Wilda shoved Behdin toward the opening and dove in after him. In a tangle of arms and legs they slid on concrete slick with slime before shooting out into another pipe.

She felt a tremble under her body. "Cover your ears!" she screamed as a wave of dust-laden hot air blasted out of the tunnel behind them.

Hanan and Henry tumbled after her. The explosion shook the walls, sucking the air from her lungs. Then they were plunged into darkness and stale air rushed in, replacing the vacuum.

Wilda coughed sand and smoke from her lungs before climbing to her feet. Around her she could hear the others doing the same. "Is everyone OK?"

"Yes," managed Behdin between coughs.

"I'm OK," added Henry from behind his helmet.

"I am fine," said Hanan holding up the glow stick. The soft light filled the chamber, illuminating the four dust-coated figures.

"Close call," she said.

"Yes," agreed Hanan. "But we can't stay here. They know we're underground now and won't stop till they kill us. We must warn the others and prepare the weapon."

"The weapon?" asked Henry.

"I will explain while we move," said Hanan as he examined the pipes running away from the junction and pointed to one. "This way."

PRIMAL 2055 – Escape

Shadow Runner, Syria

"Sir, we've detected an explosion in sector delta thirty-four," reported one of the operations officers, "and we've lost contact with two mechops and trainee Five Five."

Leon slammed both fists on the digital map. "How in god's name is she beating us?"

"This has to be that bitch Marnisha's work," said Shona from the other end of the table.

He screwed his face up. "There's no way she could influence the battlespace. She's jammed Eight Two's head full of subversive bullshit, but that isn't going to save her."

"Five Five is down, his jumper suit is requesting immediate MEDEVAC," interrupted the operations officer.

Leon stared at the red icon that denoted the explosion. Then he glanced up at Seven Nine Nine, who stood quietly in the corner. "Suit up. I want you to deliver eight mechops to the ground and evacuate Five Five."

The trainee nodded before disappearing out of the door.

"You're giving him another chance?" said Shona.

"We'll see." He turned his attention back to the map. "Show me all the tunnels that run off the origin of the detonation."

A series of routes were immediately highlighted green. Leon studied them for a moment then marked six points on the map. "Clear these areas of friendly call signs and arm the slammer pods. It's time to flush out our prey. What's the status on our flamers?"

One of the staff consulted his flexipad. "We have two in stock at the warehouse."

"Excellent, have them shipped to a holding area. Seven Nine Nine can deliver the mechops to the same location."

"Affirmative, sir."

"Slammer pods are armed," announced another officer. "Target grids uploaded."

Leon smiled. "Then let it rain."

Homs, Syria

Wilda was hunched over when she felt the first of the tremors. The sides of the narrow tunnel shook and the dull thud made her heart skip a beat.

"They're dropping bombs," said Henry wearily.

In front of them Hanan paused as another explosion sounded. This one felt closer. "They're trying to cut us off. We need to hurry."

After another ten minutes of weaving through increasingly tighter tunnels they entered one with a light in it. As they got closer Wilda made out a figure past Hanan's shoulder.

"What took you so long?" asked Eon as they arrived at an opening in the side of the tunnel.

"There were complications," said Hanan. He ducked through the breach as another rumble shook the ground.

"Yes, I heard," said Eon as he gestured for the others to follow.

Wilda led Henry and Behdin along a short tunnel before they emerged into debris-filled underground parking lot.

Soft orange light drew her eye to one corner where some of Hanan's men were gathered in a circle. They turned and greeted their leader as he approached. She spotted Behdin's sister sitting against a car to one side. The girl climbed to her feet and dashed across to greet her brother.

Wilda waited for Henry to join her. "How are you feeling?"

He slid up the helmet's faceplate, revealing his sweat-drenched features. "I won't lie, I've been better."

"How are your power levels?"

"Below thirty percent."

Eon joined them as a distant rumble shook the walls. "Come, I will show you the weapon." He led them across to where the men were gathered. The group parted revealing a partially assembled rocket surrounded by parts and tools. "This is the CHAMP."

The other men stared as Henry moved forward to inspect the weapon. "This is a Russian two twenty mil rocket." He knelt, examining the warhead. "Pretty sophisticated work you've done here. Where did you get all the parts?"

"We salvaged them from destroyed robots and other equipment."

Henry poked a circuit board. "Is that a PCY340?"

"Yes."

"Damn, I haven't seen one of those since the gen-two clankers."

"Will it work?" asked Wilda.

"No, but with the ultracapacitor from this suit I can make it work."

Wilda shook her head. "You can't leave the suit, you'll bleed out."

"It's got a small secondary capacitor. I'll survive." He glanced up at Hanan. "But the elephant in the room is how you are going to shoot it high enough."

The underground leader smiled. "That's the easy bit."

He took Wilda and Henry to the far corner of the parking lot. There, in the shadows, sat an old tank.

It was not a model that Wilda recognized. In place of the turret it sported a boxy rocket pod.

"That's a TOS," exclaimed Henry. "Gotta be over fifty years old. Does it run?"

Hanan flicked on a flashlight and illuminated the tank. "Yes, we have enough fuel to get it out onto the street." He moved around to the front of the ancient war machine. "And we have a full pod of rockets. When we launch, Sakkin will not be able to shoot them all down."

Wilda shrugged. "If you get a chance to launch them. There's an army out there and they're going to be all over this in seconds."

"Not if we use a decoy," said Henry. "If you can draw the Sakkin forces away from here then I can launch the missile."

"What! You fire the missile?" She turned to Hanan. "Can I talk to Henry alone?"

He nodded and returned to his colleagues, leaving them standing alongside the tank.

"Henry, you can't do that. The risk is too high. Even if you get the rockets away, it might not work. What's more, if it does work it's going to shut down your suit and you'll die. You need to stay underground, shielded from the blast."

Henry reached out and grasped her shoulder. "Wilda, I can make the weapon work. If you keep them off me, I'll kill the whole grid."

She felt her throat constrict. "Then you'll die."

"Once the CHAMP detonates you get me to the Sakkin facility on the western side of the city. A medical bay there is behind thirty feet of concrete. It should survive the blast."

Wilda shook her head. "No, it's too risky."

"It's our only hope. If we don't hit Sakkin head on they're going to destroy us."

She knew he was right. It was time to strike back. She stepped forward and hugged Henry through the bulk of the jumper suit. "You're the bravest man I know."

He let out a sigh as he returned the embrace. "We all pay for our sins, Wilda. My only hope is that you get out of here and make Sakkin pay for theirs."

Together they returned to the men and two siblings gathered around the rocket. The group fell silent as they arrived.

Henry stepped forward, gesturing to Eon. "You got some tools?"

The scientist nodded.

"Good, then let's get this bad boy rigged to fly."

As Henry went to work, Wilda grasped Hanan's arm and pulled him away from the group. "Using the tunnels, how far away can we get in an hour?"

His brow furrowed. "At least a mile, if they're still clear."

"Good and what weapons do you have?"

"Only what you can see."

She glanced around at the motley collection of assault rifles and rocket launchers.

"Take the railer," said Henry from where he worked.

"It's broken," she replied.

"Correction, it was broken. I re-programmed the power distributor and now it should be okay. You won't be able to use the HUD, but it does have an emergency sight."

Wilda managed a weak smile. "Great, that should help with the clankers."

"I'll help too," announced Behdin. The boy approached, cradling a Dragunov sniper rifle.

"Where did you find that?" asked Hanan with a frown.

"What does it matter? No one was using it and my father taught me."

She shook her head. "You already repaid your debt. You need to stay here with your sister."

The boy looked as if he would object, but Hanan cut him off. "You can keep the rifle if you stay to protect the others."

Behdin sighed and returned to his sister.

"How many men do you need?" asked Hanan.

Wilda shrugged. "Enough to keep Sakkin busy once Henry has the weapon ready."

He nodded. "We will take three men with us. The others will stay here to protect the CHAMP."

"We need a signal, to let us know when he's ready to launch."

Hanan took a flare from his vest and handed it to Henry. "Have someone fire this from the top of the building when you're ready."

The technician nodded then handed Wilda the repaired railer. She hefted the heavy weapon with both hands and slung it over her shoulder. Then she grasped her friend's shoulder. "We'll launch a diversion and hold them off."

He nodded. "I'll see you soon."

As they locked eyes a tear ran down Henry's cheek. She wrapped her arms around the bulky suit. "Yeah, I'll see you soon."

Chapter Sixteen

Homs, Syria

The MX22's ramp dropped and Seven Nine Nine stepped out into the darkness followed by a half-dozen of the latest generation mechops. He watched through his sensor-enhanced vision as they moved quickly to positions around the vertjet.

He paid scant attention to the other clankers that appeared, carrying a wounded member of squad *Gurion*. Instead he scanned the buildings overlooking the dusty soccer pitch that served as their insertion and evacuation point.

A flashing icon in his HUD made him aware of the arrival of the arms shipment that the Head Instructor had ordered him to meet. An autonomous truck eased to a halt a dozen yards away and a robotic arm commenced unloading weapon crates.

As he watched, an itching sensation rippled across the synthetic flesh that had patched his body. It radiated and gained in intensity, part of the healing process as the skin matured and bonded to his nerve endings. He fought the urge to rip off his jumper suit and tear at the raw flesh with his hands. Instead, he focused the agony into hatred and channeled it into a mental image of Eight Two.

"Seven Nine Nine, the casualty is loaded and the aircraft is ready for departure," announced one of the operations officer's voice in his helmet. Reluctantly he turned and stepped back onto the ramp.

The next voice belonged to the Head Instructor. "If I give you another chance, you better kill her."

He stopped. "I will, sir."

"Don't fuck this up, Crispy."

There was a moment of silence. Then the officer's voice returned. "Equip the mechops with plasma weapons and commence tunnel clearance."

Seven Nine Nine punched a gauntleted fist into the opposite glove and leaped off the ramp. As the MX22 blasted him with dust he strode toward the weapons crates that had been delivered. Popping a container he reached inside and hauled out a plasma flamer. He shrugged on the jet-black tanks and adjusted the handheld nozzle. He had trained on flamers in the simulator but never used one in real life. Designed specifically for clearing tunnels and bunkers, it shot a stream of concrete melting plasma out to a range of a hundred yards.

"Gear up," he ordered his mechops. "I'm back in business."

"This is as far as we can go." Hanan shone his glow rod on

a wall of rubble blocking their progress along a cramped tunnel.

"It's not far enough. We need to draw the clankers and hunters further away from Henry. If we don't buy him enough time to launch then..." She did not need to finish. The grim expressions the other men wore indicated they understood the price of failure.

"We could surface and move through the buildings," said Hanan. "There are other ways through the city."

"That's risky, they'll have the hunter drones searching for us," said Wilda.

He shrugged. "We've done it many times. The robots have never seen us."

"There was an access tunnel further back. Let's try that first." She pushed past the men and backtracked a dozen yards to where she had spotted the opening.

As she searched she heard a faint noise from the other end of the tunnel. Activating the flashlight on her railer she shone it into the darkness.

"What is it?" asked one of the men, his AK held ready.

"I heard a noise."

"Rats, they're as big as dogs down here."

Wilda turned her attention back to finding the side tunnel. She spotted it a few yards further along. The opening was barely higher than her knee. Squatting she shone the light inside. The slime-filled drain disappeared into the darkness.

"There's no way we will fit," said Hanan.

"I will."

"I can't let you go alone."

She shoved the railer into the opening. "Double the diversions equals double the dilemmas for Sakkin. I'll push a bit further then find a way to the surface. When the flare's launched, we'll back each other up."

"I don't like it."

Wilda pushed the weapon forward and crawled after it. "You don't have to like it. You just have to deal with it." She killed the light to conserve power. Pushing any thought of failure from her mind, she wormed her way along the tunnel.

Behind her Hanan waited a moment before leading his team back through the passageway and around a corner. As their lights disappeared into the labyrinth a faint glow appeared in another side tunnel. A figure appeared, cradling a long rifle in his arms.

Behdin stole his way along the tunnel until he reached Wilda's opening. Then he crouched and listened for the sound of her progress. When he could no longer hear the scrape of her weapon he slipped into the tunnel behind her.

Seven Nine Nine strode through the ruins of a building until he reached the location one of the hunter drones had tagged as a possible tunnel. Deactivating his helmet's sensors he inspected the opening with his single eye. It was nearly sunrise and the faint glow to the east meant he could see reasonably well.

The tunnel was concealed behind a collapsed brick wall. He hefted it effortlessly away revealing an opening. Activating the lights on his suit he illuminated the floor of the access point and smiled. The intense beam revealed boot prints in the sand.

As he stepped away from the opening he gestured for one of the new clankers to move forward. "Flame it."

To his naked eye the shimmering robot was barely visible as it made its way through the rubble. Seven Nine Nine grinned sadistically as the clanker aimed a plasma flamer into the hole. Molten plasma escaped from the nozzle with a roar, lighting up the tunnel.

He flinched as he felt the searing heat and for a split second he was back in the ambush that had incinerated his face. His limbs froze and fear washed over him while the plasma roared through the tunnel. His suit detected the change in his brain activity and dosed him with a mild sedative.

"Seven Nine Nine, what's your status?" asked an operations officer over his comms link.

Rage replaced his fear. Somehow, Eight Two had struck a blow at his very psyche. "I'm fine," he replied. "We're going to burn these bastards out."

Activating his helmet's thermal sensors he scanned the ruins around him. Glowing white patches revealed where the tunnel ran into a shattered apartment block. He smiled; all he had to do was follow the trail and burn out his prey.

Henry snapped the jumper suit's ultracapacitor into a fitting before connecting it to the CHAMP warhead. While Eon slid the unit back onto the rocket and inserted the retaining screws, Henry ran a diagnostic on his armor.

The suit was now running on reserve power. If it were in good condition it would function for up to twenty minutes. A faulty unit would drain far faster leaving Henry without mobility or critical life support.

A shout came from the tunnel they had used to enter the underground parking lot. He lifted his gaze from the touchpad on the suit's forearm and spotted one of the fighters bursting from the opening.

The stench of smoke wafted into the room as the man hunched over. "They're coming, they're coming," he managed between bouts of coughing.

Henry hefted the rocket and carried it across to the ancient tank and its boxy launcher. Eon ran ahead and climbed up at the rear of the rocket pod.

Carefully leaning the rocket against the back of the tank Henry waited for Eon to grasp it. Then he pushed it so the nose slid into one of the launcher's tubes. Sliding it home with one hand, he hauled himself higher with the other until Eon had secured the rocket and fitted its fuse.

"It's time to signal the others," said Henry as he clambered over the tank's deck to the entry hatch. Eon waved at one the fighters waiting at the tunnel entrance on the other side. The man held up the flare gun in acknowledgment but as he turned to exit there was a roar from the tunnel. Molten plasma billowed from the opening engulfing him. The remaining two fighters and the young girl sprinted in the other direction, running up the ramp toward the surface.

"We need to go!" Eon yelled.

Henry forced himself through the opening into the tank's cramped confines. He'd driven a T-72 during his time in Iraq, but that had been a fleeting experience over thirty years earlier. Now, wearing a jumper suit he almost didn't fit. Struggling past the driver's seat he squeezed himself into the control space for the rockets.

Eon followed and slammed the hatch shut. The smell of smoke and fuel hung heavy in the air as the scientist engaged the isolator switches and turned the ancient diesel engine over.

The metal beast vibrated as the starter motor whined and the cylinders knocked. Then with a sickly cough the engine roared to life.

As they rattled forward Henry studied the rocket controls. The suit's sensors detected the Cyrillic writing and displayed the translations on his HUD. A warning also flashed up, he had less than ten minutes of power left.

"We're three levels below the street," announced Eon as he skidded the tank around a tight turn.

Henry felt the nose pitch upward as they climbed.

"We need to be ready to fire as soon as we're outside." The scientist gestured to a periscope above Henry's head.

He flicked the switches that activated the rocket system. Once they were outside he would adjust it to maximum elevation and ripple fire the entire volley of twenty-four rockets. One of them would detonate high above the city and fry every electronic circuit within ten miles.

Henry exhaled as the control lights started turning green. "One last hit out for an old soldier," he murmured.

Chapter Seventeen

Homs, Syria

Wilda moved cautiously through the blackened husk of an apartment block. Out the gaping holes in the walls she could see the sun rising out to the east. It cast a soft hue across the battle-scarred city that almost made it seem peaceful.

A ball of smoke rose from the direction she had come and her heart lurched. Had Sakkin found Henry and the missile? Was he already dead?

She charged up a flight of stairs onto the roof of the building. Spinning in a circle she searched for the closest hunter drone. She spotted one a few hundred yards away, hovering above another block of apartments. Aiming her railer she balanced the red dot on the disc-shaped drone.

The weapon spun up and jolted, the recoil sharp against her shoulder. The disc bucked wildly and turned toward her. She gripped the railer and fired again. This time the penetrator tore the small aircraft from the sky, blasting it into pieces. "Now I've got your attention."

A burst of machine gun fire echoed across the city, followed by two explosions. Wilda caught a glimpse of two hunter drones streaking toward a building between her position and Henry's location. Hanan and his men had made contact with Sakkin.

The plan had been to force them to split and deal with both Wilda and the underground rebels, buying Henry the time he needed. Would they take the bait?

She checked her railer. There was only enough charge for forty more rounds; not enough when the rest of squad *Gurion* were still out there, along with all the clankers.

A dull thud reverberated through her chest as a mushroom of plasma-charged smoke billowed into the air. Hanan and his men were getting cut to pieces. She dashed back into the building, downstairs and out onto street level.

Hyper-alert her eyes searched for any sign of the shimmering mechops or ganics that stalked the streets. She spotted two in front of a gutted shop front. Skidding to a halt she raised the railer and fired.

The tungsten penetrator tore the head clean off the first clanker. A shower of sparks revealed the location of its partner.

Wilda dropped to her knee, forward rolled and fired again. Her shot hit the second mechop in the torso, severing its data lines. It fell to the ground.

She turned and took off at a sprint, ducking into a burnt out structure. Leaping over rubble and scrambling through blast holes, she put as much distance as she could between her and the destroyed clankers.

Ahead she could hear the clatter of machine guns followed by the thump of a hand grenade; some of Hanan's men were still alive. If she could get to them, maybe they could hold off the Sakkin forces long enough.

Climbing a set of stairs she dashed out onto a roof and crouched low as she made for the far edge. To her front she could see the building where Henry had been working on the tank. Smoke billowed from the structure and there was no sign of her friend.

A few blocks closer she spotted rounds striking an office block. From high on one of the floors a weapon crackled.

The gunner was a good shot and the bullets struck their target, another clanker. Wilda fired a split second before the robot did. It toppled sideways launching a plasma rocket into the ground a dozen feet in front of it.

A ball of energy flashed outward overriding the adaptive camouflage of another clanker and a ganic. As Wilda fired at them there was a roar from the distant building. Her heart soared as a wall exploded outward and the tank appeared in a cloud of dust and debris.

The armored beast turned, snorted a cloud of thick black smoke and accelerated along the street toward her. Mechops swarmed toward the tank as she pumped the trigger of her railer. From the adjacent office block Hanan and his men fired everything they had at the Sakkin forces. Their vigor was short lived. A jet of plasma lanced out from the street engulfing the building then sprayed toward the tank.

"NO!" she screamed as she spotted the clanker responsible and fired. Her round found its mark and the plasma flamer detonated in a massive ball of fire that consumed most of the street.

"Henry," she whispered as the flames rolled up into the sky leaving an oily black cloud of smoke.

Then with a roar the tank reappeared with its rubber

fittings ablaze, but the missile pod intact. It continued along the street, crushing abandoned cars as it made its escape.

She waited for the missile pod to point skyward and unleash its payload, but it never happened. Spotting a clanker giving chase she raised her weapon and fired.

The shot went wide and the robot continued to charge after the tank. It must have run out of ammunition.

"Come on Henry. Fire the damn rocket." She sprinted across the rooftop and leaped to the next building. Glancing down she saw that the clanker had reached the TOS and clambered onboard.

The hatch to the tank popped open and she saw Henry climb out. She skidded to a halt and raised her weapon. Squeezing the trigger, the railer jolted blasting the clanker back onto the dusty street.

The clanker got to its feet and staggered after the tank. As she aimed again the hairs on the back of her neck stood on end and she dove to the side. Railer penetrators blasted through the lip of the building. A chip of concrete sliced into her check and blood spurted from her face as she scrambled for cover.

"I'm sorry, Henry," she managed as she crawled away from the edge. Registering the faint whir of a hunter drone she rolled onto her back, aimed the railer and fired. The drone spun wildly out of control before crashing alongside her. Wiping the blood from her face Wilda ran toward the stairs. She needed to get onto the street and protect the tank.

Seven Nine Nine watched with disinterest as the battered armored vehicle rumbled away from him. He was fixated on a freeze frame beamed from a now destroyed drone. Eight Two was exposed. "Tree, wrap up the hostiles in the building then destroy that hunk of junk. I'm going after the bitch."

He sprinted across the road and leaped skyward, hitting the side of the building and latching onto a ledge. The suit's synthetic muscles allowed him to rapidly scale the vertical surface. When he reached the top floor he climbed in through a window.

Railer ready with combat blade extended he activated his sensors and scanned the rooms around him. Behind his faceplate, he managed a smirk. The drone had revealed that Eight Two had abandoned her jumper suit. That meant she did not have the array of sensors and weapons he had, not to mention the enhanced strength and armor.

The room he'd climbed into looked to have once been an apartment. Sand covered the skeletal remains of a couch, and faded clothing littered the floor. A child's wooden toy crunched under his boot.

Through an open door his sensors picked up a smear of heat on the wall, blood. The synthetic flesh on his face burned as he moved into the corridor, railer ready.

"I know you're in here, Eight Two. Come out and face me," his voice boomed from his helmet's speakers.

With the suit's augmented sensors he heard a scrape of metal. He raised his weapon. The air around him pulsed as he fired three rounds through cinder block walls into the source of the noise. Then he rushed around the corner.

A railer snapped and he dived to the ground as rounds stitched the walls above him, sending shock waves reflecting off the concrete. Another round slapped into the wall alongside his head. The tungsten penetrator wedged in the wall. Eight Two's railer was low on power.

Striding out into the corridor he spotted his target crouched at the far end. Eight Two fired again, her weapon coughed and he felt the penetrator hit his helmet and glance off.

"The game's over, Eight Two." He raised the faceplate. "You're going to pay for what you did to me."

A shocked look passed over her face as she saw his disfigured features.

Seven Nine Nine sprinted forward thrusting the blade on his railer out. His target dropped her weapon, slipping to the side and striking a counter blow with her combat knife. The black blade sliced through an inch of nanotube on his arm. Gripping his armor Eight Two ran up the wall and over his shoulder, landing nimbly behind him.

Cursing he spun and fired from the hip. She ducked around a corner. With his right arm hanging limply he fired round after round through the wall before giving chase.

Turning the corner he caught a glimpse of her disappearing through a door. A smear of blood on the wall told him one of his shots had found flesh. He paused to drag a gloved finger through the blood. This time it was not a ruse, she was badly wounded.

Less than half a mile away Henry clung to the side of the tank as he tried to free the rocket pod. It was jammed, unable to swivel skyward. A savage jolt almost dislodged him as Eon drove into a truck crushing the clanker that had tried to climb on board once again.

Henry faintly registered the snap of a railer as a penetrator slammed into the ancient armor. The tank lurched and spun on one track until it faced back the way it had come from. He realized that the projectile had hit Eon. The tank now headed back down the street with a dead man at the controls.

Grabbing the rocket pod he used every ounce of his remaining strength and the suit's drained batteries to tip it skyward. As he did a half crushed clanker pulled itself back onto the tank, damaged legs trailing uselessly.

"Get off my tank, ball bag," he growled and kicked it in the head. As the clanker reeled from the blow, a warning flashed in his helmet.

LOW POWER

He had a matter of seconds to launch the rockets before the suit became his coffin.

The clanker reached out and grabbed Henry's leg. He leaned over and launched blows with a savage fury that a man half his age would have been proud of. Tackling the robot he fell backward onto the deck of the tank, catapulting the clanker over him. It managed to clutch onto the front of the tank, dangling legs scraping the asphalt. For a split second it looked as if it would pull itself back on board.

Henry kicked one of its mechanical hands. "I said, get the hell off my tank!"

There was a horrendous screeching of metal as one of the clanker's legs caught in the tank's tracks, ripped the robot under and crushed it.

A final alarm sounded in Henry's helmet and his legs flopped uselessly under him. Glancing up he spotted hulking figures a short distance ahead. Railer penetrators snapped through the air, slamming into armor with a shower of sparks. He used brute strength to drag his dying body in through the tank's cupola.

He ignored Eon's corpse slumped against the controls as hypervelocity rounds tore through the armor around him. One cleaved through his chest as he reached out and slammed his palm against the launch button. He felt the tank shudder and a tremendous roar filled the air as the volley of rockets launched skyward. He managed a smile as blood spilled from his mouth and nose. "Make them pay, Wilda."

Shadow Runner, Syria

Leon managed a thin smile as he watched the feed from Seven Nine Nine's helmet cam. His trainee had come through with the goods. On screen he could see Eight Two, wounded, trapped on a rooftop.

Through his headset he heard Seven Nine Nine's voice as clearly as if he was there.

"Take it all in traitor, because this shit hole is where you're going to die," hissed the senior trainee.

A shout drew his eyes from the screen. "Sir, we've detected a launch. That TOS has fired a volley of rockets."

He frowned. "At what?"

"Can it hit us?" asked Shona from where she sat watching the final stages of the hunt for Eight Two.

"No you idiot, we're sitting at thirty thousand feet," he snapped.

"Radar track has the missiles landing less than a kilometer from their launch point," reported the officer.

A flashing icon appeared on the map and Leon checked the area around it. "The impact zone is clear?"

"Shall we engage the rockets?" asked the officer.

"No need, smoke the tank."

"Yes sir, slammer is away."

Leon turned his attention back to the feed from Seven Nine Nine. The operative was staring at the rockets flying skyward.

He keyed his headset. "Hey, Crispy. Kill the bitch."

Chapter Eighteen

Homs, Syria

Tears formed in Wilda's eyes as the rockets streaked skyward. Her gaze remained on the tank, watching it smash into an abandoned truck and finally come to a halt. "Henry," she whispered as a black dot streaked from the sky and the armored vehicle was vaporized in a flash of fire and smoke.

She swayed as a blast of hot air rocked her shattered body and she staggered.

"They're all dead. You're all alone," said Seven Nine Nine.

She clutched the bloody wound in her flank as she turned to face her executioner.

He stood a half-dozen yards away, ready to dispatch her with the blade on his railer, his molten face a mask of hatred. "Any last words?"

"You'll pay for this," she whispered.

He cupped his injured arm to his ear. "What was that?"

Her vision blurred. "People are going to make you all pay."

"Yeah, well people won't include you."

Time seemed to slow as he stepped forward, the black blade with its razor edge held high.

"I'm sorry Henry, I'm sorry mother," she murmured.

She barely registered the supersonic crack of a rifle as Seven Nine Nine staggered. Then, round after round cracked through the air, striking the Sakkin assassin.

Wilda's strength finally faded and she fell on to her back. In the sky above the city, she spotted the contrails of the rockets, thin lines reaching up into the heavens. Then there was an almighty flash and her world went black.

Shadow Runner, Syria

Thousands of feet above Wilda, on the aerostat's observation deck, Leon also saw the intense flash of light. "What the hell?" he said as the screen displaying Seven Nine Nine's helmet cam died. He spun and saw the control room's lighting flicker. Then the screens, digital maps and flight systems went blank. "What the hell was that?" he yelled.

"Sir, we've lost all power," reported one of the officers as the lights went out.

"No shit. What are you doing about it?"

Emergency lighting flickered on, revealing Shona's scared face. "What was that?"

"Some kind of EMP," snapped Leon.

"That's not possible," replied the officer. "We're shielded from EMP."

"Then what the hell was it?"

The man shook his head as he prodded at the command screens. "I don't know. Everything is offline."

"Then I suggest you find a way to fix it." The man nodded and left the command module as Leon turned his attention back to the observation deck and the city below. He spotted a faint smudge of smoke against the brown backdrop, the burning tank.

"Did Eight Two do this?" asked Shona. "Did that bitch Marnisha help her?"

Leon did not answer as he clenched the edge of the console, his knuckles white. He felt a faint shudder as the engines came back online.

"Sir, we have propulsion, but weapons and sensors are completely fried."

"Set course for the *Institute*."

"What about the trainees?" asked the man.

"Once we can communicate we'll send vertjets, till then they're on their own. Consider this part of their *Tsalmaveth*."

The officer knew better than to question his order.

Leon watched the city slowly spin under him as the airship turned. There was no doubt in his mind that Eight Two was alive and as soon as he had reinforcements, he would be back to kill her.

Homs, Syria

Seven Nine Nine clutched his pistol as he hid behind a rusted hot water tank in the basement of a store. He'd managed to free himself from the clutches of the inert jumper suit after it had been rendered useless by the blast.

The sniper who had saved Eight Two had almost killed him as he struggled to get off the rooftop and hide.

Without the suit he knew he did not stand a chance against Eight Two and her army of terrorists. He had no idea where they had come from or how they had disabled his suit. There had been no mention of resistance beyond the usual clankers and ganics in any of his briefings.

As he sat with his back against the concrete wall he fought the urge to scratch at the synthetic flesh on his face. It burned and itched, the empty eye socket convulsing along with the muscles in his torso. Without the jumper suit for cooling and pain suppression he was in a private hell.

A banging sound from above snapped him out of his self-pity and he glanced up at the ceiling, aiming his pistol at a staircase. The banging continued for a moment and then stopped. Curious he climbed to his feet and slowly edged his way up the stairs. As he crested the landing to the next floor he heard a shuffling sound from the front of the shop.

He inched forward, the pistol held ready. As he rounded the corner he spotted a crouching figure. He began to squeeze the trigger then recognized the black Sakkin uniform. It was Tree. "So you made it out alive?"

The trainee spun, holding a captured AK-47. His eyes narrowed as he took in the damage to his squad leader's face. "We thought you were dead."

"It's still early days. Do you know what's going on out there?"

Tree shook his head. "No. The clankers dropped and our suits and railers died. I managed to get out." His voice wavered. "Five Five didn't make it."

Seven Nine Nine shrugged. "We're not out of the woods yet. How did he die?"

"Some kind of terrorist army. There were half a dozen of them armed with assault rifles and rocket launchers."

"Any sign of that bitch, Eight Two?"

Tree shook his head. "No. I haven't seen her since the ambush. You think she's still alive?"

"Rats like her are hard to kill."

"What are we going to do?"

"We sit tight. Sakkin will send reinforcements. We'll RV with them and clear the city."

"What if they don't come? What if they burn the city from the air?"

The thought sent an involuntary shiver along his spine and he lifted a hand to the flesh on his face. "As soon as it's dark we'll leave the city."

"How will they find us?"

"We'll build a sign in the desert. The hunter drones will find us and we will be extracted."

"We've failed the *Tsalmaveth*, they could leave us to die here."

Seven Nine Nine made himself comfortable against the shop wall. "Leon will not leave us to die. He's lost too many of Sakkin's resources already. They'll come for us and when they do, we will have our chance to hunt Eight Two, no matter where she runs."

Chapter Nineteen

Homs, Syria

Less than a mile from where the two Sakkin trainees hid, the young woman they wanted dead lay unconscious on a makeshift stretcher. Behdin was dragging her steadily through the streets, toward the prison complex. It had been hours since the blast in the sky. Immediately after, he had heard gunfire to the west but nothing since.

Pausing in the shade of a building he lowered the stretcher and checked the casualty. Wilda was still unconscious, her breathing shallow and skin clammy with sweat.

He had bound the wound on her torso as best he could before strapping her to a sheet of carbon fiber recovered from one of the battered war machines that littered the street. He had rigged his rifle sling that let him tow the sheet like a sled. The Dragunov was tied next to her.

Confident that she was still secure he took up the sling and recommenced his journey. They had planned to all rendezvous at the prison, but Behdin had no idea how many survivors there would be. The thought of Xeyal drove him onward. He could only hope she'd stayed out of the line of fire.

As he dragged the sled around a corner he finally spotted the grey walls of the prison. The tall metal gates were wide open as he approached. Dragging the sled inside he maneuvered it down a ramp into a dark concrete-walled garage. Inside, a group of the men from the underground was helping a dozen prisoners out of their black vests.

"Behdin!" Xeyal's high-pitched voice echoed off the walls as she sprinted toward him.

He grinned broadly as she jumped into his arms. "I thought the worst."

"I knew you were alive," she said. "Those stupid robots could never kill you."

She hugged him before spotting Wilda on the sled. "Is she dead?"

"No, but she's hurt bad. I need to find a doctor."

"You need to get her as far from here as you can." The voice belonged to Hanan. The underground commander stepped forward from the group of prisoners. "They want her dead. Soon they will return with more robots, and more fire. They will burn this city to ashes to try to kill her."

"How? I can't drag her across the desert."

"This way." Hanan gestured past the prisoners to a row of tan colored military vehicles. There were tanks, trucks, pickups and a line of jeeps. "More targets for their weapons. Fortunately, they are older tech. They were not affected by the blast. We'll load them with water and food from inside and escape the city."

"Where are you going?" asked Behdin.

"My men will head south east, toward the Emirates.

There are people there that will help us fight back against Sakkin."

Behdin shook his head. "I need to take my sister home. We will travel north east, back to our village."

Hanan stared at the boy for a moment then over his shoulder to where Xeyal knelt beside Wilda. The girl had found a bottle of water and a cloth and was gently wiping the wounded teenager's face. "There are others from that region. We will prepare a vehicle and you will go together."

Behdin nodded. "We will need food and weapons."

"Yes, and we all need to move fast, before Sakkin return. Do you know where to go?"

"My father always said to follow the home star. It will lead us back to our village."

Hanan reached into the pocket of his cargo pants, removed a brass compass and placed it in Behdin's hand. "This will also help show you the way. You're a brave man, Behdin. I can trust you to keep Wilda safe."

He nodded, slipping the compass into his pocket. "We will also need medical supplies."

Hanan gestured to the small crowd of former prisoners. "There is a man here, a Kurdish doctor. He will help care for her." He grasped the teenager's hand. "Good luck, warrior."

North East Of Homs

A warm breezed kissed Wilda's cheek as she stood on a rocky outcrop gazing out over her village. The sun was setting behind a distant ridge, casting a soft glow over the shantytown. A thin haze hung over the tin-roofed houses, smoke from cooking fires where mothers prepared the evening meal for their children.

Wilda knew what would come with darkness. She had been here before, seen the destruction through the eyes of a young girl, fought back alongside her mother and watched her die, time and time again.

"Not today."

The voice came from behind, startling her. She turned to see a muscular, dark-skinned man wearing combat fatigues with a black assault rifle in his gloved hands, Henry.

"I thought I'd lost you," she said.

He gave a broad smile, eyes bright. "Takes more than a bunch of clankers to keep me down. Now, we gonna hit these suckers before they take out your village?" He gestured to their right.

Wilda followed his extended finger and spotted a convoy of trucks advancing along the valley.

"There's too many of them."

Henry snickered. "Not when you've got an army at your back."

The crunch of gravel under boots reached her ears and she turned around. Standing before her were another dozen warriors dressed in body armor and carrying an assortment of weaponry. She spotted the boy she'd befriended in the simulator among their ranks, along with the scientist who had died with Henry.

"What are your orders?" asked a voice she instantly recognized.

The crowd split and her mother appeared. Like the others, she wore fatigues and carried a weapon.

"Orders?" exclaimed Wilda. "This is all just a dream. You're all dead. Sakkin has killed each and every one of you." A twinge of pain reminded her she had been shot and she pressed a hand against her stomach. The glove came away covered in blood. "They've killed us all."

Her mother reached out and grasped her by the shoulder. Wilda gazed into her dark almond eyes and fought back tears.

"I'm so proud of you," said her mother. "You've come so far." She wrapped her arms around Wilda and hugged her. "This isn't the end, Wilda. It is the beginning. You are going to bring justice to this world. You're going to fight for all of us."

A tear ran down her cheek. "They kill everyone I love."

"We'll all be with you, Wilda." Her mother's voice grew softer, almost distant.

Darkness closed in as her mother slipped away. "Don't leave me."

"I'll never leave you," her mother said with a fading voice.

"Henry, are you there?" The darkness had closed in around her. "Is anyone there?"

She felt trapped in a dense fog.

"Hello?" her own words sounded muffled.

"I'm here. I'm with you," replied a soft voice.

Suddenly a jolt and pain replaced the sensation of loneliness. The fog seemed to cling to her vision as she struggled to focus and became aware of her body. She lay on something firm, something that bounced and jarred; a vehicle.

"Wilda, can you hear me?" The voice was louder now and familiar. She felt someone gently squeezing her hand. She opened her eyes and found herself struggling to focus on a girl's face. It belonged to Xeyal, Behdin's sister.

"Where am I?" she croaked.

"You're safe. We're crossing the desert. Behdin is taking us home."

She tried to sit, but pain shot through her torso and she slumped back onto the stretcher. Exhaling slowly, she regained control of her breathing before taking in her surroundings.

She lay in the cargo compartment of a military truck. Light shone from holes in the tattered canvas top and she caught a glimpse of blue sky. Turning her head she looked into the concerned features of Xeyal.

"I knew you would wake up," she said with a smile. "The doctor said you might not, but I knew you would." The girl passed her a bottle of water.

Wilda held it to her lips and sipped the lukewarm liquid. When she finished, Xeyal took the bottle from her. "What direction are we traveling in?"

"North east," the girl exclaimed, proudly. "Behdin, the doctor and the others have been driving."

The simple act of speaking left Wilda utterly exhausted. She fought to keep her eyes open. "Who else made it out?"

"Not many of the fighters, the man Hanan and some of his people. They saved lots of prisoners."

"What about the man in the suit?" she said. "What about Henry?"

The sad expression on the girl's face told her what she already knew. She closed her eyes, remembering her friend's smile. "I'll make them pay," she murmured as she drifted off to sleep. "I'll make them pay."

Cape Town, South African Zone

Marnisha Copeland strode through the sliding glass doors that separated Manfred Lisker's office from that of his staff.

She found the Chairman of Sakkin Industries staring out through the floor to ceiling windows at the bustling city below. He wore, as usual, an immaculately tailored three-piece suit.

"Do you ever get the feeling that they take the security we provide for granted?" he asked as she took a seat on a leather couch, crossing her legs.

"Utterly, but as long as they pay the bills, does it matter?"

An assistant entered the room and placed a tray with water and glasses on a low table.

"As fiscally ruthless as ever, my dear." He turned from the view and paced to his desk where he picked up a flexipad. "Although, the bill for your latest experiment would suggest otherwise." He glanced at the screen as he strolled around the perimeter of his expansive office. "Over three hundred million."

Marnisha shrugged. "The end was always going to justify the means."

Lisker paused and ever so slightly, cocked his head. "I was led to believe the project had failed."

Her eyes narrowed. "Who told you that? That simpleton Leon, or his whore?"

"His report indicated there was an uprising in Homs. Terrorists set off a device that shut down all of our mechops, battle suits and an aerostat."

Her brow rose. "An uprising?"

"Yes, your little project incited indigenous hostiles to fight back."

"I was assured that Homs was a sanitized training environment containing only drones and OFTs."

"Yes, well it wasn't and we subsequently lost control of the city."

"Was Eight Two terminated?" asked Marnisha.

He shook his head. "She was not amongst the bodies recovered by Leon and his team."

She took a sip from a glass.

He stared at her.

She smiled. "You wanted resourceful, empathetic operatives capable of infiltrating deep undercover. I've given you that."

"At far greater expense than was anticipated."

"The long-term value of this project is immeasurable. With this next generation of nemesis operatives, we can ensure the security of every project. We can infiltrate our enemies and destroy them from within."

"Once you work out how to control them."

Marnisha brushed a stray strand of hair from her face. "What makes you think I can't?"

"You lost control of the girl."

"Did I?"

His eyes narrowed. "You're telling me she's still operational?"

"I set her on a path. I've seen nothing to indicate that she has deviated from it."

Lisker continued his orbit of the office. "And you're confident that she will complete her mission?"

"In due course."

He reached his desk. "Time I do not have. There has been another attack in South America."

"Local trouble or Lascar?"

He snorted. "Dunbar assesses it was a local uprising." The scorn in his voice suggested he disagreed with his Head of Intelligence.

"I take it you don't concur."

Lisker removed his jacket, placed it on the back of his

chair and sat. "Tariq Ahmed has been dead for nearly a decade and still he remains a thorn in my side." He referred to the former CEO of Lascar Logistics, a man he had dealt with in his previous role as Director of Mossad's Kidon teams.

"I take it Avi's mercenaries have been unsuccessful in penetrating Abu Dhabi."

"Would I be approving the next phase of your project if they had?"

"Full funding?"

He fixed her with his steely gaze. "Full funding, I want an army of these nemesis operatives within the year."

"You won't regret this, Manfred."

"No, I won't. If it goes badly, you will." He turned his attention to the flexipad. "Now, I need to decide what to do with Leon and his squad of failures."

"It would be a waste to terminate them."

"Who said anything about termination?"

"They failed the *Tsalmaveth* and Leon allowed Eight two to escape."

"I'm not in the business of wasting company assets. They will be reassigned to Guatemala. Perhaps Leon and his prodigies can succeed where Skarvin has failed," he said, referring to his Head of Operations. "Now, if you don't mind I have other matters to attend to."

Marnisha rose and made for the door. Before she reached it, she paused and turned.

"Manfred, may I ask you a favor?"

"If you must."

"The psychologist, Shona, transfer her to the Antarctic mining project."

Lisker chuckled, shaking his head. "Remind me never to cross you, Marnisha."

A few minutes later she sat in an aircab flying away from Sakkin Headquarters toward her gated estate. As she watched sleek glass skyscrapers flash past she was filled with a sense of pride. Eight Two, or Wilda as the girl preferred, had proven to be her greatest success. Lethal, adaptable, resilient, and most importantly, empathetic, she represented the culmination of decades of research and development. She wondered where the girl was and whether she was safe. Marnisha had no children of her own. Wilda was the closest thing to a daughter she'd ever had.

Sighing she shook the thought from her head. Eight Two was an asset, not a person, a valuable asset with a significant role to play in the advancement of Sakkin Industries.

Next in the PRIMAL 2055 Series

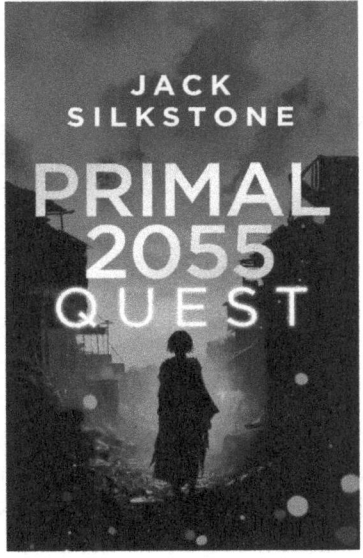

vinci-books.com/primal-2055-quest

Sanctuary is everything to Wilda, but her presence in Pendro could be its undoing.

In a world where the privileged few reign supreme, Wilda finds herself caught in the crosshairs of a looming shadow war. Seeking refuge in the Kurdish village of Pendro, she grapples with the desire to belong and the instinct to flee. As the sinister forces of Sakkin close in, Wilda must confront the consequences of her presence, knowing that her very existence endangers those she holds dear.

Turn the page for a free preview…

PRIMAL 2055 – Quest: Chapter One

Western Desert, Iraq

Wilda grimaced as she sat, bracing herself against the warm metal of the truck bed. The wound in her flank sent jolts of pain through her battered body. She sucked air through clenched teeth and slid herself to the rear of the vehicle. Swinging her feet to the ground she ignored the pain and gathered her thoughts.

It had been five days since she and the others had made their escape from the Sakkin prison in the city of Homs. Five days since Wilda, a sixteen-year-old trainee had betrayed her masters and escaped. Five days since a missile had killed her only friend, Henry.

Wiping a tear from the corner of her eye she gazed out at the horizon where the faint glow of the sun was fading. A cool breeze ruffled her hair, the first sign of another freezing night.

Moving stiffly past the truck she spotted people clustered around a small fire. The others had circled their vehicles for the night and were preparing the evening meal. Walking tentatively toward them she caught a whiff of roasting meat. The smell triggered a savage growl from her stomach.

One of them turned toward her as she hobbled closer. She saw Xeyal break away from the group with a bowl in hand. The twelve-year-old had been acting as her nurse since the small convoy had left Homs. Every time she'd woken, the girl with curly brown hair had been there to wipe her brow, wet her lips and help the doctor dress her wounds.

"Wilda, you should be resting. I was bringing you food," said Xeyal as she reached her.

"I needed to get out of that truck," she replied as she continued toward the others and the fire.

Xeyal's brother Behdin, rose from where he was sitting with his Dragunov rifle, and offered her his place on a wooden crate. Only two years older than his sister, the boy's dark eyes already bore the intensity that came from exposure to the savagery of conflict.

"How are you feeling?" he asked as she sat.

"Better."

Xeyal handed her a bowl. "You should eat. Behdin shot a goat."

Spooning the thick stew into her mouth she was pleasantly surprised by the rich flavors. "This is good," she managed between mouthfuls.

As she ate, other members of their convoy filed past the fire for a bowl of the stew. There were less than a dozen refugees, all adults, and all armed. They avoided making eye contact with her, and the ones that did wore a cautious look that bordered on fear. In their eyes, despite playing a pivotal role in their freedom, she was still a product of Sakkin, and Sakkin was the enemy.

Finishing her stew she left the fire and made her way back to the truck. Leaning against the hood she searched the northeastern horizon for an old friend. The Guardian Star was a beacon that called to her over the vastness of the desert, guiding her toward distant mountains and the facility nestled within them; the place from her dreams.

Fatigue washed over her, and she turned to the rear of the truck. Then, as she hobbled toward the tailgate, she heard something that turned her blood to ice.

The breeze carried the faint whirr of a drone's blades to her genetically enhanced ears.

"Take cover!" she screamed as her acute hearing also detected the distant roar of a vertjet.

As she dove to the ground railer projectiles slammed into the truck with a mighty clang. Then the attacking jet roared overhead and disappeared into the night. A glance toward the other vehicles confirmed they'd been immobilized in that first attack. Her training told her what would come next.

Pain shot through her body as she rose and staggered to the truck. It was still intact. Railer rounds had punched through the engine, leaving the body undamaged. Pushing aside a tattered canvas cover she reached for a crate and dragged it rearward. Inside she found the equipment that Behdin had squirreled away for her, body armor and an AKX assault rifle.

Unable to raise her left arm she lifted the armor over her head, tore the side of the vest open, and slid her right arm through the hole. Slapping the velcro closed she gripped the enhanced AK between her knees, shoved a magazine home, and racked the charging handle.

The first crackle of gunfire sounded in the desert to her

right. It was followed by the tell-tale hiss of railers and the wet slap of a human disintegrating.

Steadying the AK against the truck she scanned the sky through the weapon's enhanced optic. A fusing of thermal and night vision revealed the presence of a single Hunter drone. Sakkin operating procedures stipulated that at least one of the disc-shaped autonomous vehicles would be supporting an assault by three clankers and a ganic. Clankers, or mechops as Sakkin designated them, were robots capable of limited independent combat. Because of this they were led by a 'ganic', a highly trained human. Eliminating that individual was the most effective way to defeat a Sakkin attack. But first, she needed to deprive the assault force of their eyes.

The AKX barked twice, spitting its programmable bullets into the dark sky. Through the scope, she saw the flash of a hit and watched the drone drop.

Before it struck the ground she was on the move, hobbling alongside the truck. It wouldn't protect from Sakkin railers, but would hide her from their thermal sensors.

Crouching behind the shattered engine block she ignored the thick stench of oil and fuel as she peered around the bumper.

Her heart lurched as she spotted dark mounds where moments before people had stood eating their dinner. Beyond them she saw shadowy figures approaching, clankers. She waited till they were a short distance from the fire before she lined one up and fired. The advanced rounds punched a cluster of holes in the robot's sensor array and it blundered off at right angles to the assault.

Dropping to the ground she braced herself as a volley

of ultra high-velocity slugs rang the shattered truck like a bell.

Wilda's body was wracked with pain as she crawled away toward another truck. She'd almost reached it when the vehicle she'd left exploded in a flash of flame that lit up the sky. Debris rained down around her as she scrambled behind the remaining truck and rolled under it. Crawling to the opposite side she had a clear view of where her friends had gathered, only moments earlier.

In the flickering light of the fire she saw Behdin's lifeless eyes staring at her. She choked back tears as she searched for the enemy. A clanker appeared a mere twenty yards distant, an ominous figure that blocked the stars on the horizon.

Her AK barked as she sent a stream of armor-piercing rounds into the head of the robot. Bullets sparked against the active camouflage that cloaked the high-tech killing machine.

She changed magazines as she scrambled rearward, out from under the truck. Clambering to her feet she worked the cocking handle.

Over the low roar of a burning truck she registered the crunch of a heavy footfall behind her. Spinning she caught a glimpse of a figure before a flash of blue energy overwhelmed her vision. She lost control of her limbs as the ultrasonic wave disrupted the neurons controlling her muscles.

As she collapsed, the figure stood over her. The Sakkin operative's faceplate opened, revealing the features of someone she knew, Tree. The two of them had been trainees together. What's more, he'd once saved her life with a simple act of compassion.

"I'm sorry, Eight Two, but loose ends need to be tied up," was the last thing she heard before passing out.

When she came to she was strapped to a stretcher being loaded into an aircraft. It was the Sakkin vertjet that had strafed the convoy. She glimpsed more figures inside as her stretcher was locked into place. The ramp closed with a whine, and the aircraft lurched skyward.

"I told you I'd find you."

She instantly recognized the voice and turned her head till she faced the molten features of Sakkin trainee Seven Nine Nine.

"You killed them all," she managed between gritted teeth. "You killed them all."

He smirked. "That's just the beginning, Eight Two."

He disappeared, and for a few minutes she felt the aircraft bank and weave before it slowed then touched down.

Wilda's heart raced as two mechops carried her stretcher clear of the aircraft, and into a building she recognized. She'd seen it over and over in her dreams. It was the hospital where she'd been born.

Her stretcher was transferred to a gurney, and she was wheeled along a corridor, through several sliding doors into a brightly lit room.

Figures gathered around, and a machine hummed as a clamp grasped either side of her head.

"Welcome home," said a feminine voice. A face appeared in front of Wilda, the beautiful elfin features of a woman she'd seen once before, inside the Sakkin training facility.

"Why am I here?" Wilda asked. "Why not kill me with the others?"

The woman smiled. "Because my dear child, you have

something that belongs to us." The buzzing of a machine gained in intensity. She struggled to move her head. Cold metal touched the side of her temple, followed by intense pain as it commenced drilling into her skull.

Wilda's screams echoed off the walls of the facility as she thrashed against her restraints. Then, as the medical tool punched through her skull, she fell still.

Village of Pendro, Kurdistan

Wilda clapped a hand to the side of her head as she sat upright, heart racing. Pain shot across her body, and she slumped back onto the bed, breathing heavily.

She wasn't in the hands of Sakkin, her friends weren't dead, and no one was drilling into her skull. Instead, she was lying injured in a stone shepherd's hut on the outskirts of Behdin and Xeyal's village.

Unlike the dream, their convoy had crossed the desert without being attacked. Behdin's story of their escape from Sakkin had ensured his family welcomed her, but the other villagers kept their distance. She didn't blame them. Life in the Morass was hard, and strangers couldn't always be trusted, especially ones linked to the forces that abducted their children.

Exhaling, she fought through the pain in her side as she slid off the mattress onto her knees. Leaning on the wall she made it to her feet and stood for a moment in the darkness.

The wound she'd sustained in combat with Seven Nine Nine should have killed her. Fighting on a rubble-strewn rooftop in Homs, a railer bolt had ripped through her torso, ripping muscles and devastating organs. However, somehow her body had been able to keep her alive and repair. She suspected it had something to do with the treatment she'd received in the *Institute*. Sakkin Industries had led the world in genetic research and manipulation. It made sense that their ganics would be enhanced. The thought sent a shiver up her spine as she wondered how much of her the corporation had changed.

Wilda felt along the wall until she found her jacket. Shrugging it on she found the walking stick that Behdin had carved for her and pushed open the rickety wooden door.

Icy wind whipped her hair as she scanned the darkness. The faintest glow of light from the east told her it was early morning. At least a dozen lights flickered from the village, a few hundred yards away. The people of Pendro were early risers.

She heard a faint cry from Behdin and Xeyal's house, fifty yards distant. Light shone from the girl's room. There wasn't a night that the child didn't wake screaming. Her dreams were every bit as real as Wilda's. It broke her heart that she couldn't help, but only a mother's embrace could soothe the child's anguish.

Behind the hut was a path that led up into the rocky slopes of a mountain range. She hiked it most mornings, in the hope it would help rehabilitate her wounded body. It also gave her time away from the village to think and, more importantly, remember.

Branches and thorns scraped at the shoulders of her jacket as she followed the goat trail through thick bushes. As she climbed, she wondered how dark it was to people without genetic enhancement. On the journey across the desert, she'd realized she could see details that Behdin, Xeyal and the others couldn't.

When she finally reached the edge of the thicket she

glanced up at the mountain. Toward the peak, the first rays of sunrise cast a wide swath of light across the craggy landscape.

She climbed a few hundred feet to an outcrop that overlooked the valley, and lowered herself gently onto a boulder. This was the part of the day she loved the most. Training underground in the Sakkin facility called the *Institute*, it was rare for Wilda to see the sun, let alone watch it rise over a majestic mountain range and spread its warmth across a fertile valley.

The village was nothing like she had expected. The lessons she'd received at the *Institute* painted a very different picture of the region. The morass, as the broader Middle East was now called, was supposed to be a barren and desolate wasteland populated by marauding tribes of criminals and terrorists. Yet, below her, nestled between rugged ridges was a thriving community of families living peacefully.

A tear traced a path down her cheek as she thought how much Henry would have loved it here. The Sakkin technician had longed to be part of a family, to be surrounded by people who loved and cared for each other. He'd given his life so that Wilda and the others could be free. That was a sacrifice she would never forget.

Leaving the outcrop she followed a ridgeline a little higher. The sun was on her back now, she could almost feel its healing powers flowing through her battered body.

She paused at the point where the ridge joined the bulk of the mountain. Here the goat track split. The path she usually took went right, dropping back down to the village. The other went left and wound its way higher. In the dozen times she'd walked the trail she'd never gone left. However, today something drew her in that direction, and she hobbled along the path as it wove between outcrops of granite.

As the climb got her blood pumping, the wound in her side throbbed. It gained intensity as she pressed on, savoring the pain. It reminded her that despite Sakkin's best efforts, she was still human.

She reached a steep ravine where the wind was howling, and realized she couldn't go any further. The trail descended steeply, impassable in her injured state. Frustrated, she turned and started back toward the village.

She took a few paces then paused as she heard something from the canyon. At first, she thought it was the howl of the wind rushing between boulders, but then it gained in intensity, the distraught wail of an animal in need.

Returning to the ravine she peered down into the rocks and bushes. The wailing noise continued, louder now, a forlorn cry from what she could only assume was a dog.

Throwing caution to the wind she started down the steep slope. Digging her walking stick into the gravel she used it as an anchor to control her descent. Halfway, she paused and listened.

A long drawn out howl confirmed that the dog was in a cluster of boulders a dozen feet below, surrounded by thick thorns. Sliding slowly she found a tunnel that animals had burrowed through the bushes. Thorns snagged her clothes, and her wounds sent pain shooting through her body as she crawled inside.

As she approached, the wail of the trapped animal intensified. The sound led her to a narrow gap in the rocks. Peering into the dark space she spotted the animal wedged between two boulders. It was a small dog with caramel-colored fur and black ears.

"Hey, it's going to be OK, little guy," she murmured as

she reached down and grabbed him by the scruff of his neck. He hung limp as she plucked him from the crevice and placed him on the ground.

She'd never seen a dog like this before. The animals that wandered the streets during training had all looked alike, long-legged and lean with pointy ears. This one was small and chunky with floppy black ears, a short snout and curled up tail. Creases on his forehead made him look like he was permanently frowning.

Wilda held her hand out the dog and he gave it a tentative sniff before licking her. "You're welcome," she said.

Feeling somewhat elated by her successful rescue mission Wilda crawled out of the bushes and made her way slowly up the slope. Stopping to let the pain subside she turned back and saw that the dog was following her. She waited as he scrambled up the hill and stood a few feet away, watching her.

In the soft morning light she could see grey around his muzzle and wisdom in his eyes.

"Going my way?" she asked.

He cocked his head sideways before scrabbling up the rocks to the trail above. There he sat and turned back as if to tell her he was waiting.

"Oh, it's going to be like that, is it?" She half expected the dog to stay with her for a short distance before returning to his home. He definitely wasn't from the village. Their dogs were like the ones in Syria. However, once she'd reached the mountain trail, he tagged along, seemingly content with her tortoise-like pace.

A half-hour later, as she emerged from the thorn bushes that bordered the shepherd's hut, she spotted Behdin sitting on a rock.

"Good morning. Father has invited you to join us for

breakfast," he said when she was closer. "Did you go for a walk?"

"Up the hill a little." She paused to catch her breath.

"Is it getting better?" he asked?

"Slowly."

The Kurdish teenager peered past her into the bushes. "Is that a dog?"

Wilda turned and saw that the little hound was standing at the edge of the thorn bushes. "I found him in the hills. If he follows me home, I can keep him, right?"

Behdin nodded. "As long as he doesn't chase the goats. He looks hungry. You should bring him to breakfast."

"He might tag along."

It was a short walk through the fields to Behdin's family home. Constructed from thick mud bricks, it had a flat roof made from a mixture of iron and solar panels. It was a cozy four-room residence where Behdin lived with his father, mother and sister Xeyal. They'd offered her one of their rooms, but she insisted on staying in the shepherd's hut. It would make leaving that little bit less painful if she could slip away in the night. Additionally, if Sakkin made their move before she was healed, they might grab her and spare the others.

As they approached, the rich smells of the breakfast that Behdin's mother, Serav, was cooking hit Wilda's nose, and her stomach growled.

"Was that the dog?" Behdin asked with a chuckle as he opened a wooden gate and waited for Wilda to enter. She stepped through and turned to see if the dog would follow. The small hound paused a half dozen feet from the wall.

"Come on then," he said.

The dog didn't move.

"I think he's happy there." Wilda followed Behdin

through the family's lush vegetable garden into the courtyard. In the summer months they usually cooked and ate their meals here, on a sturdy wooden table under a canopy of vines.

"Good morning!" Behdin's younger sister Xeyal jumped up from the table and launched herself at Wilda.

She braced herself, but the teenager hugged her gently.

"Are you feeling better?" asked the children's mother as they sat. Serav passed Wilda a plate of cold meat, boiled eggs and greens. Her husband, Haval, joined them at the table.

She smiled. "I'm getting there."

"Wilda found a little dog on her walk," said Behdin.

"A dog," exclaimed Xeyal. "Where is it?"

"He's outside the gate," he said. "I'll show you."

The curly-haired girl and her brother dashed from the table.

Haval shook his head. "Those two! Wilda, you should not go too far from the village. There are raiders and bandits in the hills."

"I'll be careful."

"Careful is not enough. Don't go into the hills alone." Like most of the villagers, Haval found it hard to comprehend their stories of Sakkin robots and airships. He assumed Behdin and Xeyal had been abducted by raiders.

"What are you doing today, dear?" Serav asked her husband, redirecting his attention.

"Working on the water purifier. The stream will dry up soon, and the bore water is salty."

"If you can't fix it, what will happen to my garden?"

"It will die, and we will starve."

Haval finished his breakfast and rose from the table as Behdin and Xeyal returned.

"He's so cute," the girl gushed.

"But he won't come closer," added her brother.

"Put some food out and give him some time," said their father as he kissed his wife on the cheek. "I will see you for lunch."

"Wilda, would you like to help me in the garden?" asked Serav, once her husband had left.

"Yes, I'd like that."

"Can we help too?" asked Xeyal.

"No." Her mother chuckled as she cleared the table. "The two of you need to go to school."

"That's so unfair," said Behdin. "How come Wilda doesn't have to go to school?"

"Because something tells me that Wilda has learned more than enough hard lessons for one lifetime."

PRIMAL 2055 – Quest: Chapter Two

Los Angeles Enclave, North America

Manfred Lisker wasn't a man used to sitting in the wings. The CEO of a billion-dollar security firm, he was accustomed to being the most important person in the room. However, when it came to the Sumsunto corporation, he didn't rate a seat at the table. The six men and two women who surrounded the polished thousand-year-old Californian Redwood table were some of the most influential people on the planet. They controlled the resources, food and equipment that the isolated enclaves of the Advanced Block (**ADBLOK**) required to survive and thrive. There were other corporations, but Sumsunto was largest and, as such, was Sakkin Industries' most important client.

The meeting was one that occurred every financial quarter, and Lisker's presence was testament to the fact that his people were critical to Sumsunto's dominance of global manufacturing. Sakkin Industries provided security for the corporation's mining and agriculture activities outside of the safety of the ADBLOK. Over two-thirds of his workforce, trads, ganics and clankers, was committed to their largest client.

"That brings us to the next point," spoke the American at the head of the table. The eighty-year-old Sumsunto chairman looked barely middle-aged with smooth skin and piercing blue eyes. "Rare earth minerals."

From his chair at the rear of the room Lisker's ears pricked at the mention of the ultra-expensive commodity. REMs were the critical component in Sumsunto's manufacturing of fusion reactors, and underpinned their delivery of technology to the ADBLOK. He knew for a fact that the Chinese mines were nearing depletion. They needed to find a new supply, and that might come with additional opportunities for Sakkin.

Sumsunto's head of resource procurement took his cue from the chairman and began speaking, "Initial surveys indicate significant deposits of REM located in eastern Turkey and Northern Iraq."

"Kurdistan!" exclaimed another official. "You want to mine in the morass?"

Lisker suppressed a smile. The morass was the name given to the region formerly known as the Middle East. Devastated by conflict, it was a wildland of tribes, shattered cities and irradiated ruins, the perfect environment for Sakkin to capture a lucrative security contract.

"Yes," continued the resource chief. "Unless you know of a REM deposit somewhere else, perhaps here in California?" His sarcasm silenced the other man. "I'm seeking a budget to conduct further exploration."

The chairman nodded. "Manfred, is it really that bad?"

Lisker rose as he straightened his jacket. "The tribes and criminal elements in that region are well equipped and organized. They will pose a significant threat to any mining operations. However, Sakkin Industries have several assets in the area, including a forward operating base where we've been conducting operations to destabilize criminal elements."

"Would it take much for you to expand your operations?" asked the resource chief.

Lisker shrugged. "If we want to control the area, we need to ensure the tribes remain fractured. That will require additional resources."

"Go away and crunch your numbers and come back with a price," said the chairman. He turned to the resource chief. "How much do you need for initial scoping and planning?"

"That depends on—"

"A number, give me a damn number."

"Ah, thirty million."

"Approved." He rose from the table. "That concludes our business. Manfred, I appreciate you and your people making the trip." With that, one of the most powerful men on the planet departed the conference room, followed by three executive assistants.

The other attendees of the meeting followed suit, except for the resource chief who made a beeline for Manfred. "How long will it take you to develop a plan?"

He stood. "I'll have something to you within forty-eight hours."

"Excellent." The executive shot Manfred thumbs up before following the others out of the room.

Alone Manfred gazed out through the windows at the

vast metropolis of Los Angeles. Once dominated by sprawling ghettos, traffic, and pollution, the enclave was now a vista of glass, water and greenery. The city of twenty million souls represented the apex of modern civilization. Since Sumsunto perfected miniature cold fusion in 2036, and led the push for California to secede from the United States, LA had emerged as a cutting-edge tech enclave.

Protected from the outside world by walls, drones and Sakkin security forces, inhabitants lived exceptionally long and healthy lives, oblivious to the suffering, fear and hate that were rife in the outside world. He liked to think of the populace below as sheep and Sakkin as the sheepdog that kept them safe. There were wolves beyond the green pastures, and it was their job to hunt them down and kill them.

Leaving the conference room he rode a high-speed elevator to the roof of Sumsunto tower, where his aircraft was waiting. The sleek grey vertjet was the fastest and most comfortable in the Sakkin fleet. The size of a medium business jet it had stubby wings that ended in ion thrusters. Autonomous and capable of vertical flight, like a helicopter, it covered the distance between LA and Sakkin's HQ in Cape Town in less than six hours.

The craft's side door was open, and he stepped into the luxury interior, handing his coat to a waiting assistant. Making his way aft, he joined two other men already seated in plush leather chairs.

Avi Lerner and Dominik Skarvin were dressed similarly to Manfred, expensive well-cut suits and crisp white shirts. Both, like him, were former intelligence officers who'd swapped their national loyalty for money and the luxuries that came with it.

"How did it go?" asked Avi Lerner, Sakkin's Head of Covert Operations, as his boss sat.

"Very well."

The aircraft trembled as Manfred fastened his seatbelt. Silently it lifted into the air, turned slowly and accelerated. They climbed smoothly as the jet transitioned from vertical lift to forward flight, taking less than a minute to reach cruising altitude.

Manfred exhaled as he unfastened his belt. Takeoff in the vertjets always made him slightly uneasy. A stewardess appeared with a glass of his favorite single-malt whiskey on ice. He took the glass and sipped the golden liquid, savoring the burn as it slid down his throat. "How many men do we have in Kurdistan?" he asked Avi.

"At the Proteus facility?"

"Yes."

"Just the one operative, Yitzhak." Avi took his drink from the waiter, a gin and tonic. Dominik, Head of Operations, already had one in hand.

"Yitzhak Gorahn, I remember when that old dog was running Kurdish rebels into Iran. I can't believe he's still around."

"He joined us after Jericho," said Avi, referring to the nuclear detonation that had triggered the greater middle-eastern conflict and the destruction of Israel, Iran, Jordan, Lebanon and what remained of Syria.

"He knew the region, so I put him into Kurdistan in case we ever needed to operate there. He's been playing the tribes off against each other for over a decade now."

"Excellent foresight. Sumsunto has discovered rare earth minerals in the area. We need to develop a plan to secure both their exploration and future mining operations. I want to lead with clandestine activities before expanding into conventional security operations."

"We can leverage off Yitzhak's work and base out of the Proteus facility."

"Then we can increase our footprint with additional ganics and mechops," added Dominik in his thick South African accent. "There is already a small contingent at that facility."

Lisker nodded. "I'll speak to Marnisha Copeland."

"Is she going to have a problem with this?" asked Avi.

"No, merely a formality. She's been running a new lab in Rwanda, the Kurdish facility is scheduled for closure." He took another sip of whiskey. "Does Lascar have a presence in the area?"

"Not that I'm aware of."

Dominik shook his head and snickered.

Avi shot him a dirty look.

Lascar was an organization that worked outside the ADBLOK. Officially they distributed humanitarian aid and supplies. From Lisker's point of view they were a criminal entity, and were known to support tribal terrorist elements. They were a thorn in Lisker's side that, so far, his head of clandestine operations had been unable to mitigate.

"This is a massive opportunity for us. Lascar, or anyone else, cannot be allowed to jeopardize it."

"Then I need additional resources to target them," said Avi.

Lisker's eyes narrowed. "If we can secure Sumsunto's rare earth supply, funding will not be a problem. You will both have what you need to destroy Lascar and anyone else who gets in our way."

Turkey-Kurdistan Border Region

The sniper made a slight adjustment to his scope, sharpening his view of the drone. The boxy craft hovered, its pulse engines stripping the ground below it of dust and debris.

"What is it doing?" asked his partner, laying alongside, peering through a pair of binoculars.

They were hidden on a rocky slope a short distance from where the car-sized autonomous aircraft was stationary above the valley floor.

"Masrour says it is checking for minerals."

"It can do that without landing?"

"It would seem so. Confirm range and windage."

"Five-hundred and twenty yards, wind running from two o'clock at three knots."

At that range the wind would have minimal impact on the twenty-millimeter ultra high-velocity projectile loaded into the breech of his weapon.

He exhaled slowly as he gently squeezed the trigger. The key to accuracy with a rifle this large was to not anticipate the violence that was about to be unleashed.

As the firing pin smashed into the primer the propellant ignited, accelerating a bullet larger than his finger to over four-thousand feet per second. He'd barely registered the brutal buck of the compensated recoil when his spotter reported a strike. Working the bolt he chambered another round and reacquired the target.

The drone wouldn't need another. His shot had hit the propulsion system, delivering sixty-thousand foot pounds of energy into the ion thrusters. It fell to the ground in a smoking and spluttering heap.

"Target destroyed," reported his spotter.

It took them less than thirty seconds to break down the heavy rifle and abandon their position. Making their way down the mountain they were met by a battered pickup.

"Good shooting," yelled the driver, through his open window.

The two men climbed into the bed and the truck took off along the valley floor in a cloud of dust. It skidded to a halt twenty yards from the downed drone.

The sniper grabbed an axe, slid from the bed and ran to the shattered body of the aircraft. With rapid blows, the hardened steel sliced through aluminum, carbon fiber and plastic revealing the innards of the million-dollar robot.

"You found it?" his spotter asked.

"This is it." He used the blade of the axe to pry a component the size of a handheld radio from its fixtures. Handing the axe to his partner, he wiggled a dozen cables from their sockets and pulled his prize free. "Let's go."

As the truck bounced along the valley floor he examined the cold metal box. There were characters engraved on the side, a nonsensical jumble of letters and numbers that would mean something to the technicians. He pondered the fact that something so small could be so valuable. Four separate teams had watched different valleys for the chance to a down a drone. Their commander, Masrour, had promised the successful team a reward of ten goats. The animals would go a long way to feeding his family of six.

He cradled the box the entire three-hour journey from the valley back to his hometown. Then, on the outskirts of town, he carried it deep into an abandoned mine, the stronghold of the Barzani militia.

"Well done, Razim," said his commander, Masrour as he took the device. "You have certainly earned your prize."

The sniper watched with interest as Masrour took the

device to a man he had not seen before. Razim knew a warrior when he saw one, and the stranger may have been hunched over a computer, but he looked like a soldier. He peered over so he could see what was happening with the device.

"The computer is encrypted," said the man.

"Can we get in?" asked Masrour.

He shook his head. "No, but we can access the location data storage in the navigation system. That will tell you where the drone has been."

"Revealing the areas that could be targeted by mining operations."

"Correct."

The stranger tapped his fingers on a tablet as Masrour and Razim watched. A moment later he handed the commander the tablet. "They've been busy. This survey drone has covered most of your territory and the surrounding tribal areas. I've seen similar activity in a number of regions."

"What happens next?" asked Razim.

"They move their equipment in and poison your land."

"We will fight back."

"You can't do it alone," said the man.

"The Barzani does not need allies," snapped Masrour. "We need more weapons."

Village of Pendro, Kurdistan

Wilda inhaled deeply as she burrowed her hands into the peaty soil of one of the raised garden beds. The earthy odor was comforting, but at the same time somewhat alien. Dust, blood, smoke and burning fuel were the scents that marked her childhood. Time in Serav's garden allowed her to escape from those memories.

Placing the seedling Serav had given her into a hole, she packed earth around it then lifted a watering can. There was a soft growl from behind as she poured. Turning, she saw that her new friend, the small brown dog, was facing the gate with his hackles raised.

"What's up?" she asked as she lowered the can.

The dog shot her a concerned look before fixing his attention back to the gate.

A moment later a figure appeared on the other side of the barrier. It belonged to Palin, whose mother was the tribal chief, and father the head of police. Tall with an athletic build and brooding good looks, he had shown a lot of interest in her since she'd arrived.

"Doing a little gardening?" he asked.

Wilda nodded as she reached for her walking stick.

He made to enter the garden but stopped when the dog growled. "Who's this little guy?"

"He doesn't have a name yet," said Wilda as she approached the dog. Ignoring the pain as she knelt, she offered the dog her hand and was rewarded with a sniff and a lick.

"He looks vicious," he said, sarcastically.

She gently placed a hand on the dog's head and stroked his soft black ears. "Looks can be deceiving."

"True." His eyes narrowed. "How are your wounds? You seem a lot more mobile."

"I'm good." Wilda gave the animal one last pat. "I've got a lot to plant, so I'm going to get back to it."

"So, no plans to move on?"

She rose and turned to face him. He met her gaze with crossed arms.

"Wilda, where are you?" The shout came from the village side of the garden. Xeyal appeared and stepped past Palin, pushing open the gate. "Where's the dog?" she asked. "Is he still here?"

"I missed you too," responded Wilda, with a laugh.

Behdin wasn't far behind his sister and confronted Palin at the gate. "Why are you here?"

"I was checking on our guest."

"And?"

"She seems to be doing well. Behdin, Xeyal, good to see you. Please give my best to your parents. I'm sure I'll see them at tonight's meeting."

Wilda watched him walk away. "Tonight's meeting?" she asked Behdin as he joined them in the garden.

"There's a big feast. Other tribes have sent their chiefs to talk."

"About what?"

He shrugged. "We'll find out when we go."

"We?"

"Yes, everyone is invited."

"Wilda, you have to come," said Xeyal from where she was attempting to coax the dog out from behind a stack of firewood.

"I think it's better if I stay here with the dog."

"You should come," said Behdin. "You're part of our tribe now. The dog will be fine without you."

"He needs a name," said Xeyal. "We can't keep calling him dog."

Wilda didn't expect the feeling of belonging that swept over her as she limped across to where the girl was kneeling.

She'd only experienced it once before, that she could remember. It had been when a broken old warrior had given her a name.

"I think we should call him Henry."

Grab your copy...
vinci-books.com/primal-2055-quest

About the Author

Jack Silkstone grew up on a steady diet of Tom Clancy, James Bond, Jason Bourne, *Commando* comics, and the original first-person shooters, *Wolfenstein* and *Doom*. His background includes a career in military intelligence and special operations, working alongside some of the world's most elite units. His love of action-adventure stories, his military background, and his real-world experiences combined to inspire the no-holds-barred PRIMAL series.

www.ingramcontent.com/pod-product-compliance
Ingram Content Group UK Ltd.
Pitfield, Milton Keynes, MK11 3LW, UK
UKHW040119190326
469155UK00004B/1242